As soon as she'd finished checking the valves, Sydney started up the stairs to the helipad at a dead run. She could hear Dixon breathing hard through the comm. He sounded like he might need backup.

When she reached the top of the stairs, she saw Weiss leap from the copter and run toward the two men. She had her automatic out, but Weiss was in the way of her shot. She ran toward the struggle, gun ready.

Blake swung the heavy wrench, catching Weiss in the shoulder and sending him careening into Dixon. Seizing the opportunity, Blake pulled an automatic from his waist and dashed for the helicopter.

Still sitting in the back of the helicopter, Marshall was focused on the monitors in front of him and the instructions coming over his headphones from Pensacola. He looked up as the vibration of the motor changed and suddenly found himself staring at the business end of an automatic weapon, and a glowering stranger.

Unable to get a clear shot, Sydney tried to run after Blake, but he was already in the pilot's seat and spinning the rotors for takeoff.

She leveled the gun at Blake as he lifted from the platform, then she stopped. *I can't shoot*, she thought. *Marshall is still on board!*

The 430 ro   sped away.

The helicop   cked.

D0684734

14

ALIAS™

THE
apo™
SERIES

STRATEGIC RESERVE

ALIAS™

THE
apo™
SERIES

STRATEGIC RESERVE

BY CHRISTINA F. YORK

An original novel based on the
hit TV series created by J. J. Abrams

SSE

SIMON SPOTLIGHT ENTERTAINMENT

New York   London   Toronto   Sydney

AS ALWAYS, TO STEVE, WHO MAKES EVERY DAY AN ADVENTURE.

AND TO SHANE AND LYNETTE, WHO TAUGHT ME FIRSTHAND
ABOUT THE PERILS OF PARENTHOOD.

SSE

SIMON SPOTLIGHT ENTERTAINMENT
An imprint of Simon & Schuster
1230 Avenue of the Americas, New York, New York 10020
Text and cover art copyright © 2006 by Touchstone Television.
All rights reserved, including the right of reproduction in whole or
in part in any form.
SIMON SPOTLIGHT ENTERTAINMENT and related logo are trade-
marks of Simon & Schuster, Inc.
Manufactured in the United States of America
First Edition 10   9   8   7   6   5   4   3   2   1
Library of Congress Control Number 2005933334
ISBN-13: 978-1-4169-0946-0
ISBN-10: 1-4169-0946-X

ACKNOWLEDGMENTS

In the course of writing this book I spent a great deal of time researching locations. I visited dozens of Web sites, looked at hundreds of pictures, and read thousands of words. Each one contributed something, some detail or clue that helped me understand the places I wrote about. To each and every one of the people behind those sites, I owe a debt of gratitude for sharing their adventures with me and, through me, my readers.

I have lost track of all the sites I visited. Some contributed a single image; some, like the Aleyeska Pipeline site, I returned to again and again for background information. They all proved invaluable. My thanks also to Jim York, father-in-law and friend, for his help with helicopters and drilling platforms. I hope I have used everyone's information well, but in the end, any errors or omissions are mine.

In addition, I want to thank the other people that made this book possible. Patrick Price, a great editor who gave me the opportunity; Jodi Reamer, part agent, part guardian angel; Jim Caldwell, a boss who understands when a deadline means taking vacation days to write; and the Hilltop Irregulars, who are always ready with support and encouragement.

CHAPTER 1

PETROLEUM ASSOCIATES DRILLING PLATFORM
GULF OF MEXICO
APPROXIMATELY 100 MILES SOUTH OF
MOBILE BAY

From the helicopter ten miles out the drilling platform looked like nothing more than a gray bump on the glistening blue horizon of the Gulf of Mexico.

Behind pilot Eric Weiss, Sydney Bristow and Marcus Dixon sat in a pair of forward-facing seats. As Weiss effortlessly flew the Bell 430 helicopter, they reviewed their plans one last time.

Sydney, a tall attractive woman in her early thirties, was dressed in a tailored black pantsuit, a starched white shirt buttoned to the collar, and low-heeled boots. Her dark hair was pulled back

1

tightly and wound into a knot at the base of her neck. Thick-framed glasses were perched on the bridge of her narrow nose, giving her the look of a rather harsh librarian. The only chink in her severe demeanor was a tiny daisy-shaped rhinestone pin on the lapel of her jacket.

Dixon, a solidly built African-American man in a conservative dark suit and tie, spoke to the other agents through his headset, in order to be heard over the noise of the helicopter. "The platform's chief engineer, who reported the spill, is expecting us. His name's"—he checked his notes—"Jack Clark. You heard the tape, Sydney. He didn't say it, but he clearly suspects sabotage."

Sydney nodded, then spoke for the benefit of Jack Bristow and Michael Vaughn, at their monitoring station near Pensacola, Florida. "Got it." She glanced at the clipboard of papers she carried with her. "You take the files, I'll check the production level."

"Right," Dixon said. "Merlin, are you ready to scan the platform?"

Behind them Marshall Flinkman sat motionless, his back to the cabin. He stared intently at a bank of computer monitors. Marshall tapped at his keyboard, paused to scan an on-screen report, then entered another sequence of commands.

"Shotgun," he said, speaking to Vaughn over his radio, "this is Merlin. This puppy looks solid as a rock. I mean, if there was a rock anchored to the bottom of the ocean, this would be that solid, if you—"

Marshall stopped, listening to a reply through his headphones. "Yes, sir. Of course, sir. I just meant, uh—what I was saying was—no, sir, no signs of structural damage."

In her headset Sydney heard the voice of her father. "Outrigger," Jack addressed Dixon, "this is Raptor. You are go for the mission."

By now the platform was much closer, and a lot bigger. Sydney could clearly see the helipad standing over what looked like a giant stack of shipping containers, with ladders running down the sides.

As they landed, Dixon spoke again. "This should only take about twenty minutes." He nodded toward Weiss. "Keep the engine warm. And, Marshall, let us know if you see anything out of the ordinary. Raptor," he continued, "this is Outrigger. Phoenix and I are in play." He nodded to Sydney, and the two of them removed their headsets and stepped down from the craft.

To Sydney's surprise the wind atop the drilling rig was no more than a mild breeze. Once clear of the rotor wash, it barely lifted the escaped tendril of hair that tickled her neck. She tucked the errant strand behind her ear and followed Dixon across the platform.

At the side of the deck, near the metal ladder, a man waited, glancing at his watch. Impatience seemed to ooze from him, like sweat from his pores.

As they approached, Dixon reached into the inside pocket of his suit coat and produced a badge. He held it in front of the man's face, then flipped it back into his pocket. "Frank Morris, EPA. And you're Jack Clark, the chief engineer?" He extended his hand to Clark and cocked his head in Sydney's direction. "This is Missy Baxter, my assistant."

"Glad you got here so quick," Clark said in a thick Southern drawl, taking Dixon's hand. "Corporate's been heating up the phone lines, asking when we can bring the rig back online. Keep reminding me how much money we're losing every minute we aren't pumping."

Sydney stepped forward, angling the flower pin on her lapel toward Clark and offering her hand. She smiled at Clark and held his hand for a fraction of a second longer than an average handshake. The warmth of the gesture was not lost on Clark.

On her comm, which was well hidden by the heavy frames of her glasses, she heard Vaughn speaking from Pensacola. "This is Shotgun. We have his image, Phoenix."

Sydney released Clark's hand but held him with her smile. "We understand, Mr. Clark. Really, we do." Her voice carried a hint of Georgia, and the dimple in her left cheek winked at the engineer. She started toward the ladder. "The oil supply is very important to national security. We want to get you back up and running just as quick as we can."

Clark smiled back. Clearly, this charming Southern girl understood the urgency of bringing the platform back online. He led the two visitors—he could hardly think of them as investigators when they were being so helpful—down the ladder from the platform to the crew quarters, where his office was.

Sydney paused as she started down the steps. The view was spectacular, and she wished she could take the time to enjoy it. That was one of the problems with her job: There was never any downtime. Spies, it seemed, didn't get coffee breaks.

Although thousands of gallons of crude oil passed through the platform every day, all Sydney could smell was the sharp tang of salt water, carried from the ocean a dozen floors below.

Clark opened a door on the first landing and led them into the crew quarters. They walked down a long hall dotted with doors on either side.

"Bunk rooms," Clark explained. "Because of the shutdown, most of the crew are home, taking advantage of the time with their families—those of them who have families. We only have a skeleton crew on the rig. I still can't believe that any of them could be deliberately involved in this, whatever it is."

Even though Clark had reported his suspicions, he seemed to be backpedaling, trying to wish away his fears. "It has to be some kind of innocent mistake, or a mechanical failure I couldn't find," he went on.

He turned a corner, and the hall widened into a large dining room, filled with utilitarian folding tables and straight-backed chairs. On the opposite side of the room the hallway continued. "The offices are down there," Clark said, gesturing toward the back of the room. "And here are the elevators to the production deck." He turned to Dixon. "That's what you want to see, right?"

"Actually, we'd like to see the maintenance logs first," Dixon answered.

Clark shrugged and led them across the hallway to an office, where he opened a lateral file cabinet and pointed to a neat row of loose-leaf binders. "Daily logs, maintenance records, manual and automated sensor logs. It's all here."

Dixon picked up the daily logbook for the current month and skimmed through the pages. Beside him Sydney took notes. The whole time she was hunched over her clipboard, her lapel was pointed toward the pages of the book.

"Good, Phoenix," Vaughn whispered in her ear. "A little to the right." Sydney stretched, as though easing a cramp in her neck. "I got it, thanks."

"Missy," Dixon said, "would you take a look at these three valves, please?" He pointed to the page and a list of locations, and Sydney quickly copied the information onto her notepad. "I need to ask Mr. Clark a few questions, and then I'll be right down."

Clark registered surprise, clearly expecting the charming Southern girl to be a secretary, not an engineer, but he quickly masked his reaction.

Sydney left the room and hurried to the elevator, knowing Dixon would keep Clark occupied while she checked out the production floor away from Clark's prying eyes.

One flight down she crossed the production level and passed through the firewall. The leak in the pipeline that had triggered the shutdown could have been caused by tampering anywhere along the line. It was as good a place as any to start.

Clark had certainly meant what he said about a skeleton crew. Syd hadn't seen anyone since she left Clark and Dixon. As she walked toward the wellheads, she asked quietly, "Are you getting all this, Shotgun?"

"Affirmative, Phoenix," came the reply. "This is Raptor. Shotgun's on the phone with Sloane."

Sydney winced at the name of her boss, Arvin Sloane. She had only animosity for the man who had been responsible for so many deaths. Even though the director of the CIA had pardoned him, *she* could not forgive him.

There were too many lost friends, and family members, in Sloane's wake.

"Phoenix, this is Raptor." It was her father again. "Is everything all right?"

"Fine, Raptor. Just—" She stopped suddenly. There was someone else on the production floor, bending over one of the wellheads with a pipe wrench as long as Sydney's arm. "Somebody's down here," she whispered.

All Sydney could see was a broad back in a short-sleeved blue work shirt. The fabric was taut against slabs of muscle, and his sleeves strained around his arms.

The man turned and spotted Sydney. She could see the name "Blake" stenciled across the left side of his shirt. He gave her an innocent smile, and turned back to the wellhead.

"He saw me," she said. "Looks like he's working on one of the wellheads."

Sydney heard Dixon speak up through his comm. "Are you doing any work on the rig now, Mr. Clark?"

She couldn't hear Clark's reply, but Dixon repeated it for his listeners. "So, there isn't any maintenance scheduled until our assessment is complete?" he confirmed.

"Be careful, Phoenix," Raptor said in her ear. "There shouldn't be anyone on that level."

Sydney watched as Blake moved away from the wellhead and around the firewall.

"He's walking away," Sydney said. She

watched for a moment, not moving. "He's taking the stairs, not the elevator."

"This is Raptor, Phoenix. Check that wellhead; see what he was up to. Outrigger, move to intercept him at the stairs."

Sydney could hear Blake as he took the steps two at a time, his work boots pounding up the stairs. He didn't pause at the landings but kept climbing at a quick pace toward the top level of the crew quarters.

Sydney ran through the field of wellheads to the spot where she had first seen Blake. She couldn't remember exactly which wellhead he had been touching.

"Raptor, this is Phoenix. Can you see the wellheads? There are at least five he could have tampered with over here."

"This is Merlin, Phoenix. Shotgun's feeding me the visual in the chopper. There's an access plate on the base of the wellhead, to your left. There will be tool marks on the screw heads if it's been opened."

Sydney knelt on the floor and bent down, examining the access plate. "Negative, Merlin. I'll check the next one."

While she checked the wellheads, Dixon emerged onto the first-level landing. Above him Blake was sprinting up the last flight of steps, his gaze turned toward the sound of the idling helicopter on the helipad above.

Too late to cut off his target, Dixon broke into a run, charging up the stairs behind the fleeing man. At the top of the last flight of steps Blake looked back over his shoulder, as though realizing for the first time that he was being pursued.

As Dixon reached for his weapon, Blake charged him, knocking him to the ground. Although he was well trained and in superb physical condition, Dixon was no match for the mountain of muscle in the blue shirt.

Sydney heard Dixon's grunt as he hit the ground, but she couldn't leave the wellheads until she was sure they were safe.

"Merlin, I'm not seeing any marks," she said. "What next?"

"Check the valves. They should be closed tight."

She grabbed the nearest control wheel and yanked hard. It didn't budge. She quickly checked each of the other valves in the area. They were all tight.

"All secure, Merlin."

Inside the helicopter Weiss listened to the exchange over the comm. Looking from Marshall back to the platform, he saw that Dixon was down.

"Stay here," he yelled at Marshall, and ran to Dixon's aid.

As soon as she'd finished checking the valves, Sydney started up the stairs to the helipad at a dead run. She could hear Dixon breathing hard through the comm. He sounded like he might need backup.

When she reached the top of the stairs, she saw Weiss leap from the copter and run toward the two men. She had her automatic drawn, but Weiss was in the way of her shot. She ran toward the struggle, gun ready.

Blake swung the heavy wrench, catching Weiss in the shoulder and sending him careening into Dixon. Seizing the opportunity, Blake pulled an automatic from his waist and dashed for the helicopter.

Still sitting in the back of the helicopter, Marshall was focused on the monitors in front of him and the instructions coming over his headphones from Pensacola. He looked up as the vibration of the motor changed and suddenly found himself staring at the business end of an automatic weapon, and a glowering stranger.

Unable to get a clear shot, Sydney tried to run after Blake, but he was already in the pilot's seat and spinning the rotors for takeoff.

She leveled the gun at Blake as he lifted from the platform, then she stopped. *I can't shoot,* she thought. *Marshall is still on board!*

The 430 rose into the air, turned north, and sped away.

The helicopter, and Marshall, had just been hijacked.

"Outrigger? Phoenix? Do you copy?" Jack's voice rose in frustration as his best friend and his daughter failed to answer him. "Phoenix?"

"Here, Raptor."

Jack hid his relief from the men with him. "Don't let them see you sweat" were words he lived by.

"He got away, Raptor," Sydney said. "He took the copter, with Merlin still aboard. He's heading north."

"Copy that, Phoenix. Merlin has activated the locator beacon, and we're tracking the copter. We'll send another copter for you. In the meantime find out who the hijacker is, and bring his records with you."

CHAPTER 2

GULF SANDS AMUSEMENT PARK
FLORIDA PANHANDLE

The line for the Scenic Helicopter Ride stretched from the gate at the edge of the helipad and around three sides of the small square of asphalt. Sunburned families enjoying their vacations waited impatiently to fork over their thirty-five dollars each and take a ten-minute tour of the beach.

A helicopter appeared on the horizon, headed for the landing pad. Although the previous flight had taken off only three minutes earlier, the teenage couple at the front of the line smiled. They'd had a feeling that the kid ahead of them would throw a tantrum and the copter would be back faster than usual. The young man swallowed the last sip of his lukewarm soda and reached for the gate.

The copter was coming in fast. Much faster than it had on the previous flights. The tourist hesitated, apprehension winding through his gut.

As the copter set down, he backed up a step, bumping into his girlfriend, who was close behind him. The craft that had just landed clearly wasn't a tour helicopter.

Vaughn watched in frustration from the copilot seat of another Bell 430 as the stolen craft from the drilling platform touched down on the tiny pad at the amusement park.

The pad was too small to land a second copter, and the crowd was too thick for them to land anywhere else. All he could do was watch as the broad back of the man known only as Blake emerged from the helicopter on the ground. Vaughn was close enough to see the automatic in his hand.

The crowd moved back, parents shielding their children behind them, as Blake ran across the landing pad, vaulted the fence, and headed for the center of the busy amusement park.

"Follow him!" Vaughn yelled at the pilot. "Raptor," he said into his comm, "the target is headed into the park. We are in pursuit, but there's no clear place to set down."

"Stay on him, Shotgun," Jack replied.

Below them Blake pushed through the crowd. He knocked aside a large woman in a tropical print dress. The woman's male companion made an attempt to threaten Blake, then threw his hands up and backed away when Blake turned the automatic on him.

Although Vaughn couldn't hear their voices over the roar of the engine and the thumping of the rotors, he could see panic beginning to sweep through the crowd.

Blake plowed forward, sending children running as their frantic parents scrambled to pull them from his path.

"I have to get down there," Vaughn shouted at the pilot.

The pilot shrugged. There was nowhere to put down without endangering a lot of bystanders.

Too impatient to wait any longer, Vaughn released his harness and moved between the seats. He pulled a safety line from the bulkhead.

Securing one end of the line to a cleat in the floor, he opened the door and tossed the other end out. The pilot veered to the left, whipping the rope behind him, narrowly avoiding tangling it in a giant Ferris wheel.

"Get me as close as you can," Vaughn said. He snapped the line into a descender on his flight suit and positioned himself at the open door.

They continued moving, following Blake's progress through the park. Vaughn waited, poised to jump, as they banked around a whirling octopus, then rose quickly to clear the top of a roller coaster.

Blake ran around the coaster, and Vaughn saw a chance to get ahead of him. He signaled to the pilot, who dropped down nearer the ground on the far side of the ride.

The crowd scrambled away from the descending craft, creating a small clearing.

"Shotgun is in play," Vaughn said, and jumped. The rope slipped through the descender, and in seconds he was a few feet above ground, surrounded by stunned tourists. He hit the quick release and dropped the last few feet, landing in a crouch.

He stood up, looking around for any sign of

Blake. To his left he heard shouts, and then a single gunshot.

The crowd surged away from the sound of the shot, moving toward Vaughn, who forced his way against the tide of frightened vacationers. Vaughn tried to fight his way forward, but the panicked crowd was relentless, and every time he shoved past a wall of screaming tourists, another group got in his way.

At last Vaughn came to the fence marking the perimeter of the park. Beyond the fence was a private beach, quiet and serene, that bordered the elegant facade of an expensive waterfront hotel. He looked around frantically, but he knew he was too late.

Blake was gone.

Behind Vaughn the panic of the crowd eased and families reunited as the immediate danger seemed to have passed. Small groups huddled together, adults comforting crying children. But farther away Vaughn could hear the tidal wave of panic still moving through the park.

Blake had left injury and fear in his wake, and then disappeared. There was no sign of the fleeing hijacker.

Vaughn looked up at the helicopter hovering above him and addressed the pilot. "You see anything?"

"Negative. No sign of him," the pilot responded.

"This is Shotgun," Vaughn said into his comm. "I've lost him."

Vaughn ran back through the park, anger and frustration burning through him. Blake had hijacked a helicopter, kidnapped Marshall, frightened innocent vacationers, and fired into a crowd of bystanders. And he had gotten away.

People moved out of Vaughn's way and let him pass. It was as though his anger was burning a path through the crowd. Soon he reached the helipad, where he found a traffic jam of helicopters. The excursion pilot had returned to find his pad occupied, and was hovering a few yards offshore. Another copter, carrying the team from the oil platform, was circling the nearby parking lot.

Vaughn's pilot, meanwhile, radioed that he was returning to base, easing the congestion only slightly. Vaughn was relieved to find Marshall standing next to the grounded copter, running his fingers through his dark hair.

"I swear, there was nothing I could do," he said when Vaughn approached. "I don't know how to fly a helicopter. I mean, I know how to fly it—it's a simple matter of physics and rotational torque—but I've never *actually* flown one, and I really didn't think it was a good time to try. . . ." Vaughn was so glad to find Marshall unharmed that he barely registered the incessant rambling.

Sydney, Dixon, and Weiss ran up to join them. Their rented copter had found a small opening in the parking lot and let them off. Now it, too, was returning to base.

From above, the excursion pilot motioned frantically and buzzed the group of agents.

Marshall looked up and caught an unmistakable single-fingered salute from the pilot. "We ought to get out of here. That guy doesn't look too happy, if you know what I mean. In fact, I think he is definitely unhappy."

Weiss nodded and signaled to the rest of the team to follow him. He strapped into the pilot's seat of their original 430, with Dixon in the seat next to him.

Behind them, in the seat next to Sydney, Vaughn donned his headset and spoke over the roar of the rotors. "Swing around the park. I lost the guy in the crowd, but we can't leave without looking one more time."

Weiss nodded.

"Houdini, this is Raptor." Jack's voice was harsh in their headsets. "He's long gone. Bring the team back to base. Now."

"Yes, sir." Weiss turned sharply and headed for the rendezvous. There wasn't anything more APO could do at the park.

Sydney watched Vaughn clench his fists. She imagined she could hear his knuckles popping from the strain.

Oblivious to the others, Marshall sat facing his monitors, back in his safe techno-geek world. "I was sure glad to see you guys," he said as they headed for home. "I mean, my wife would have killed me if I had gotten killed on a mission. Of course, I would already be dead, so she couldn't *really* kill me, but she'd be really upset. And she would definitely kill me if she got the chance."

From his seat next to Weiss, Dixon clamped his jaw tight and listened, trying to control his guilt. He was the one who had let Blake get away in the first place, the one who had put Marshall in jeopardy.

I'm not going to let it happen again, he vowed silently.

APO HEADQUARTERS
LOS ANGELES

Sydney stared across the conference table at Arvin Sloane. Even though he was in charge of APO, she still didn't entirely trust the man. He had changed sides too many times, betrayed too many people.

It didn't help that he was chewing out Michael Vaughn in front of the rest of the team. Her sister, Nadia, still on assignment in Taiwan, was the only one spared the discomfort of watching Sloane lay into the agent.

"You mean to tell me, Agent Vaughn, that you simply lost the man in the crowd?" Sloane asked. His voice was icy.

"When I got close, he fired. There were too many civilians for me to return fire, and in the resulting panic he just disappeared," Vaughn said, slapping the table on the last word.

Marcus Dixon spoke up. "I—we—don't think the platform was the primary target." He passed around a sheaf of papers, topped by copies of Blake's picture. "According to the company's files, Blake had access to most of the rig. If he had wanted to, he could have done a lot more damage."

"Dixon's right. The damage was minor," Sydney added. "I talked with Mr. Clark while we were waiting for our pickup. When Blake took off, Clark got a lot more talkative. He admitted that he thought the pipeline had been sabotaged. I believe his exact words were, 'There's no way this could have been an accident.'"

"It appears that Mr. Clark's employer wanted to handle the investigation internally," Dixon went on. "They didn't want any publicity, and they seemed to think the best way to do that was to have their own security personnel investigate. Clark thought his job might be endangered by calling the EPA, but his engineer's license was on the line if he didn't."

"He was right to call us," Jack Bristow said. "Oil production is a matter of national security. If someone is trying to sabotage that platform, we need to know about it."

"That's true," Sydney said. "But when Clark and I examined the wellhead, it didn't appear that Blake had done anything to it. However, we went over as much of the rig as we could, and we did find this." Sydney pointed to a spot on one of the photographs in her copy of the mission report. "These tool marks on the crude oil cooler. Clark says nobody should have touched the cooler. We believe the cooler was opened, allowing the saboteur access to the pipeline. Whether to put something in or take something out, Clark couldn't say."

"I didn't have time for an extensive analysis," Marshall said. "But I did do a preliminary review of the scans we took. They were of the pipeline itself, and of course the visual data that Sydney got while she was inspecting the wellheads and the crude oil cooler—which, by the way, was a fascinating piece of machinery. It has—" He stopped himself from going off on a tangent as both Sloane and Jack glowered at him.

"Anyway," Marshall said, waving away his diversion and returning to the mission objective, "the point is, we made scans of the pipeline, and it appears that some kind of foreign object passed through it shortly before the leak was discovered. I can't tell which direction it was traveling yet, though we can assume that it followed the flow of the oil from the platform to the shore. We're checking on that now."

Vaughn shook his head. "I still can't believe that

guy dumped the helicopter. I mean, he could have gotten miles away, and instead he put down the minute he reached land? We were incredibly lucky to get the copter, and Marshall, back so easily."

Marshall nodded his agreement, acknowledging Vaughn's unspoken concern for his safety. They knew this was a dangerous business, but it didn't stop them from caring about what happened to their fellow agents.

"It was hardly luck, Agent Vaughn," Sloane said. He leaned forward, reasserting his control over the briefing. "That aircraft is large and valuable and not easily hidden. In addition, it has a tracking device capable of disclosing its location at all times. He knew we'd track him down no matter what. Blake abandoned the copter at the first opportunity. Mr. Flinkman, as valuable as he is to us, was merely an impediment to Mr. Blake. One thing is clear. Whoever is behind this has a long-range goal. And we need to find out what it is."

Around the table each agent waited expectantly. Clearly, Sloane had information, and probably a plan.

"There is a rumor in the financial markets that Global Oil, in Nigeria, is buying up marginal oil fields. Global is a major player, and these fields don't fit their usual acquisitions. It appears that Global is playing a game we don't recognize, and I don't believe it's a coincidence that an oil platform was sabotaged at the same time that this is occurring. Dixon, you and Sydney are going to Nigeria. Once there, you will infiltrate Global Oil headquarters. We need to know if there is a link between Global and Blake, and if Global is involved in the attempt to sabotage the Petroleum Associates platform. Jack, you will be their backup in Nigeria. Wheels up in three hours. Marshall, you will continue your analysis of the data from the pipeline. Hopefully, you will be able to determine what went through that line, where it came from, and how the damage was caused. Are there any questions?"

Around the table the agents shook their heads and gathered up their reports.

Sydney hurried to her desk, glancing at Nadia's empty desk as she passed. For most of her life she hadn't even known she had a sister; now she missed her when she wasn't around.

But Sydney didn't have time to think about that now. She had a plane to catch.

Dixon, heading for his own desk, took a detour

and went into Marshall's office instead. He had put Marshall in danger, and he couldn't shake the guilt he felt.

The tiny space was jammed with technical gear, and monitors flashed continuously. Marshall, however, wasn't watching the monitors. Dixon paused in the doorway before stepping into the cluttered office. "You okay, Marshall?" he finally asked.

"I'm fine. Really. A little rattled from all the excitement, but it's better than sitting around here, isn't it? Fieldwork and all that. It's what this job's about. Right?" This was typical Marshall banter, but the usual cheery rambling sounded hollow, as though something important were missing. And Marshall seemed distracted, compulsively looking around his office. He didn't meet Dixon's gaze.

Dixon watched Marshall with concern. He was a brilliant engineer, capable of cracking the most sophisticated locks and data encryption. Even under intense pressure Marshall could pull off amazing feats of code breaking. But this had been different.

After a moment Dixon realized what Marshall was looking at. All over his office, pinned and taped to every surface, were pictures of his wife, and of Mitchell, his son. The cheery toddler, blessed with Marshall's unwavering optimism, smiled out at Dixon from every panel. It reminded Dixon of his own two children. They might be teenagers now, but he remembered when they were small and how anxious he always was to see them after a mission, to reassure himself that they were safe, no matter what dangers he had faced.

"Go home, Marshall," Dixon said, pushing aside the rest of his questions. "And give Mitchell a hug for me."

Marshall grinned and grabbed his jacket. "I'll do that."

From the hallway Jack Bristow watched their exchange. Although he couldn't hear the conversation, he could sense Dixon's concern. As Dixon turned to leave the office, Jack quickly walked away.

SYDNEY BRISTOW'S HOME LOS ANGELES

The house was quiet when Sydney unlocked her front door. Inside, everything was in order. No dirty dishes left in the sink, no clutter in the living room.

The beds were made, and the bathroom sparkled with cleanliness.

It was as if nobody really lived there.

There was more truth to that statement than Syd wanted to think about. Even with Nadia living with her, they were gone more than they were home, one or both of them constantly off on a mission, leaving the house empty.

The demands of their jobs, the sudden trips and constant uncertainty, didn't allow room for pets. Sydney noticed a drooping houseplant. She couldn't even take care of a fern.

As Sydney took a suitcase from the closet, the phone rang.

"Hello?"

"Hi." It was Nadia. "I just wanted to see how you were. I'm on my way back. I should be home in a few hours."

Sydney sighed. "I'm fine. I wish I was going to be here, but I'm leaving for Nigeria in an hour. . . ." Her voice trailed off.

"I know. You'll be gone before I get home," Nadia said. Sydney could hear a faint smile in her sister's lightly accented voice. She could imagine Nadia shrugging her shoulders—this was all par for the course. "I'll see you when you get back. Have a safe trip."

Sydney hung up the phone, missing her sister more than ever. As she went to pack, she wondered what it would be like to have a normal life, complete with a regular family. Someday, with luck, she just might find out.

CHAPTER 3

GLOBAL OIL COMPANY
LAGOS, NIGERIA

Dixon strode through the tall glass door and into the sleek steel and glass lobby of the four-story Global Oil headquarters, which was located on the west end of Lagos Island. He wore a Muslim robe and cap. Beside him Sydney was clad in a dark purple hand-embroidered jilbaab, the traditional Muslim long dress, and a hijab, or head scarf. Both agents carried understated but expensive leather briefcases.

"Half the country is Muslim," Dixon reminded her.

Sydney nodded. The dress covered her from

33

chin to heel, concealing her tightly muscled body. She looked like many of the women on the streets of Lagos; no one would notice her.

They approached the reception desk, where a young man greeted them. "Welcome to Global Oil. I am Mr. Dako. How may I help you?"

Dixon spoke in the cultured tones of an Ivy Leaguer. "I'm Horace Cathcart, from Star Petroleum, here to see Mr. Tombiri. I have a three o'clock appointment." He pulled back the cuff of his robe, ostentatiously consulting the Rolex on his left wrist. He knew the watch would read 2:45. He also knew that Tombiri was out of the country, spending a few days on the Amalfi Coast with his latest "personal assistant."

A frown creased Dako's forehead. "I am so sorry. Mr. Tombiri is not in, Mr. Cathcart. I do not believe he was expecting any visitors today."

"But I have an appointment! Are you sure he is not here?" Dixon took on a tone of injured dignity, and drew himself up straight. It was an imposing sight.

"Yes, sir. But I would be happy to consult with his personal secretary, if you wouldn't mind waiting a minute." Dako gestured toward a sleek leather sofa in the waiting area.

Dixon nodded. "Please," he said. "I have come a long way for this meeting."

"Of course." Dako reached for a telephone, then pointedly waited until Dixon and Sydney moved out of earshot.

Sydney set her briefcase by her feet, moving it slightly from time to time, as though unable to sit still. A tiny camera concealed near the hinge recorded the movement of the elevators and the activity around the reception desk.

A few minutes later the receptionist motioned to Dixon, and they again approached his desk.

"I am so sorry, Mr. Cathcart. It appears that Mr. Tombiri is out of the country, and is not expected back for several days. Perhaps if you could tell me the nature of your business, I could reschedule you with another of our representatives."

Dixon frowned and cleared his throat. He pitched his voice slightly higher, allowing a note of distress to show through. "This is highly unusual. We had an appointment to discuss an extremely confidential matter. I don't see how anyone else would do. Is it possible you or I could speak to Mr. Tombiri on the telephone? Perhaps he could offer some solution."

Dako struggled to conceal his discomfort, but

Dixon simply waited. Beside him Sydney held her breath as the silence stretched and the tension grew.

Finally, Dixon shook his head. "It is clear that you are unable to make that decision on your own." He nodded toward the chair where he had been sitting. "My colleague and I will be happy to wait while you consult your superiors." His tone indicated that anyone would be superior to the useless Mr. Dako.

With an imperious nod, Dixon returned to his seat, keeping an eye on Dako.

Sydney followed Dixon, once again positioning her briefcase to record the activity around the reception area. After a few moments, she rose from her seat, leaving the briefcase in place.

"I'm going to the ladies' room," she said to Dixon, speaking softly enough to seem dainty, yet loud enough for Dako to hear. "I'll be right back."

"Ten minutes," he grunted, glancing at his watch. The gesture wasn't lost on Dako, who was furiously punching buttons on his phone, trying to find someone to help him handle the situation.

Sydney made a show of consulting the building directory before moving across the lobby. She turned into a short hallway lined with photographs of Global Oil installations around the world. She passed a small commissary, where a bank of vending machines offered bad coffee and unhealthy snacks. *Some things are truly universal*, she thought.

The next door bore a plaque of the silhouette of a woman. She opened the door and slipped inside.

A thin, blond woman in a Western-style business suit and pumps was washing her hands. She nodded at Sydney.

Sydney nodded back and walked slowly into the stall at the far end of the room. She waited a few seconds, listening as the woman's heels clicked across the tile, and the door opened and closed behind her. Syd peered through the crack between the door and the stall, making sure she was alone.

High above her was a grate covering a ventilation duct. Moving quickly, Sydney stripped off the jilbaab and hijab, revealing a black, skin-tight jumpsuit. Around her waist, where it had been concealed by the flowing jilbaab, she wore a webbed belt with flat pockets.

From one pocket she extracted a narrow blade.

Standing on the toilet, she fitted the blade into the screws holding the grate and quickly extracted four of the six screws.

The bathroom door clicked as someone turned the handle. Sydney jumped down and sat on the toilet, her feet clearly visible beneath the stall door. Her heart was beating fast, and she concentrated on controlling her breathing.

Two women came in, chattering in a local dialect. From their conversation she deduced that they were secretaries exchanging gossip. Sydney counted the seconds until they were gone, the scent of cheap perfume lingering after them.

As soon as she was sure she was alone, she went back to work on the grate. Within seconds she had removed the last of the screws. She put the grate and her discarded clothing inside the opening of the hatch, then pulled herself up into the duct.

She looked at her watch.

Four minutes left.

The schematics Marshall had provided showed a maze of tunnels throughout the building. Normal access to the upper floors was restricted, and there was no way she could move between floors without being heard. But she could reach the first-floor security office.

She crawled as quickly as she could, twisting along the narrow channel. Refrigerated air flowed past her from the building's central cooling system, sending chills down her body. She hurried toward her destination.

One last turn and she was in the duct above the security monitoring station. Through the grate she could see a guard watching the monitors, and another hanging a heavy ring of keys in a cabinet.

She took a miniature transmitter from her belt and positioned it on the floor of the duct, facing the bank of video monitors and computer screens. The transmitter looked like an ordinary screwdriver, the kind a careless workman might have left in the duct the last time it was cleaned.

For the next twelve hours, APO would have both video and audio surveillance of the security office. By the time the batteries died, Sydney and Dixon would be safely back in Los Angeles.

Two minutes left.

Sydney slid back along the route she had come, moving as fast as she could without making a sound. She reached the duct that led to the women's room with less than a minute to spare.

She could hear voices in the room as she approached the grate. The secretaries were back; one of them was in tears.

Sydney watched, her frustration mounting, as the seconds ticked past. Moving with extreme care, she managed to place the hijab back on her head.

The crying woman continued to sob as her friend tried in vain to comfort her.

Ten seconds left.

A third woman entered the room. Her authoritative tone made it apparent that she was the two secretaries' supervisor. After a few sharp words, the three women left.

Sydney moved the grate and dropped to the floor. She shoved the grate back into place and spun in two screws. There was no time for the rest. If anyone noticed they would just assume some maintenance worker had been too lazy to finish the job.

As she emerged from the women's room, she passed the two secretaries and their supervisor, now huddled in an angry knot in the corridor outside the commissary.

One of the women shot Sydney a quizzical glance, but her attention immediately returned to her boss. It would be days later before she recalled the strange woman who had appeared out of nowhere.

Back in the lobby, she saw that Dixon had returned to the reception desk, and was once again confronting Dako.

"Is there no one who can handle this?" Dixon asked, his voice exasperated. "This is outrageous!"

Sydney stepped in beside Dixon.

"Perhaps," she said, addressing Dixon in an accent that matched his own, "we could arrange a later meeting?" She turned to the receptionist. "Do you know when Mr. Tombiri is expected to return?"

"It may be several days, I am told."

Sydney drew her brows together slightly, letting a tiny furrow of concern appear for a moment. "Perhaps a video conference, then, with Mr. Tombiri and another representative of your firm. Could that be arranged any sooner?"

"Perhaps," Dako replied, clearly distressed that the visitors weren't taking no for an answer and going away.

"That's good, then," Dixon said. He paused, his face thoughtful, before continuing. "We can return tomorrow at eleven o'clock." He spoke with finality, as though the matter was settled.

That was Sydney's signal. It was time to leave.

"Thank you, Mr. Dako. We will return tomorrow morning," she said.

Dixon and Sydney walked swiftly away from Dako, before he could suggest another day or time. By eleven o'clock the next morning they intended to be far away from Global Oil, and from Lagos.

Two blocks later the "couple" turned into the ornate lobby of a waterfront hotel. Moving with a self-assurance that deflected curiosity, they crossed the lobby, passed the gift shop, and disappeared.

Minutes later Sydney emerged in a flowing white pantsuit and oversize sunglasses, her hair loose around her shoulders. She carried a soft-sided leather tote.

Sydney and Dixon watched as the cleaning crew exited the building via the back door to the Global Oil headquarters. From their vantage point concealed behind the loading dock of a nearby building, they had watched the crew enter just after dark. A directional microphone had picked up the crew's chatter as well as the electronic blips and beeps that had opened the unmarked door, which were uplinked to Marshall at APO headquarters.

The agents knew the layout of the building from studying the blueprints. As lights went on and off, marking the crew's progress, they compared the activity to the schedule APO had pulled from the cleaning company's database.

They had also learned that the main computer center was on the third floor, and confirmed this information by checking it against the recordings from their visit earlier that day. As they watched the building they saw that no lights came on in that area. The cleaning crew was not authorized to enter the computer room; only Global employees with the highest security clearance were allowed on that floor.

While Marshall worked feverishly at headquarters, decoding the lock sequence and encoding a transmission that would repeat it, Sydney and Dixon monitored the building, waiting as the crew disappeared into the darkness. Finally the last workers went home.

"Raptor, this is Outrigger. Phoenix and I are in play," Dixon announced.

Sydney and Dixon moved silently through the shadows at the back of the buildings. When they were in position, Sydney held a receiver against the keypad that activated the lock.

"Merlin, the receiver is in place."

"Roger that, Phoenix." Marshall tapped a few keys on his laptop. "Sending the signal now."

Marshall pushed one last key, sending data flashing across his screen. He watched as the code was transmitted and then as it sent back confirmation of each pulse. "Phoenix, you should have access in five . . . four . . . three . . . two . . ."

Halfway around the globe from where the code was cracked, the lock gave a quiet click and a tiny green light blinked on above the door handle.

"Thanks, Merlin. We're going in," Sydney said.

"Good luck," Marshall answered.

Dixon crouched beside the door as Sydney pulled it open just far enough for him to slide through. Sydney followed him in, gently pulling the heavy door closed behind her. The lock clicked into place, echoing through the silent service corridor.

Marshall had only had time to decrypt three computer system passwords before going to work on the door codes. Sydney hoped that would be enough.

The corridor was pitch black, and Dixon stopped

to let his eyes adjust. He looked around carefully, listening for activity. Satisfied the room was empty, he motioned for Sydney to move forward.

They crept down the corridor to the stairway. Their soft-soled boots made no sound on the bare metal treads as they ascended, and they moved swiftly in the dim security lighting in the stairwell. At the third floor landing they paused. According to the plans the stairs continued for another flight, dead-ending at an access hatch leading to the roof.

"Outrigger, Phoenix, this is Merlin. We have one heat signature approaching your location."

The two agents crouched in opposite corners of the landing, weapons trained on the door, as Marshall continued to feed information into their headsets.

Nearby, Jack listened to the same information. He waited, ready to come to the aid of his daughter and Dixon if they called for backup.

Sydney heard the jangle of keys on the other side of the door to the stairwell, but the door remained closed.

"Looks like a routine patrol," Marshall said. "He's headed for the elevators." There was a pause, then he continued. "He's moving up, stopping on the next floor. Which makes sense, since there's only one floor above you. Anyway, it looks like he's getting out of the elevator up there. You're clear to move in."

Dixon covered Sydney as she disabled the lock on the door and stepped into the corridor, then followed her into the hall. Outside the third door on their left a security card reader guarded a blank door.

Dixon took a key card from a pocket in his jumpsuit. It was a copy of one of Tombiri's cards. The executive had left it tossed carelessly on the dresser of his hotel room in Amalfi, and an ally of APO had borrowed it.

Dixon slid the card through the reader, and the door clicked open. So far everything was going according to plan. He waited next to the door, guarding their escape route, as Sydney crossed the room and approached a partitioned cubicle. The nameplate next to the opening identified it as the desk of the chief information officer. She took a small electronic device from her pack and plugged it into a port on the side of the computer. "Merlin," she said, "the package is in place."

"Got it, Phoenix. Now type in this code."

Marshall read her a string of letters and numbers, the first of the passwords he had decoded.

Sydney typed as he read, reading the characters back to him in a low voice.

For a few agonizing seconds nothing happened. Then the screen flashed red and a message appeared: Incorrect password.

"That one didn't work, Merlin," she said.

"Okay, let's try the next one," Marshall said. He read another string of numbers, with the same result.

When the third code didn't work, Sydney could hear the tension in Marshall's voice. "Give me a minute, Phoenix, while I decrypt another password. I have about twenty of them, I just didn't have time to do them all before we got the door codes, and then the doors took a while—"

"This is Outrigger. Do we have anything on that heat signature you picked up?" Dixon broke in.

"Hold on, Outrigger." There was a buzz of background conversation at headquarters, then Marshall answered. "He appears to be on the roof. No, he's moving. Looks like he's coming back down the stairs." He paused, and Sydney could hear him muttering.

"Wait, wait, wait! I think I have an idea here,

Phoenix. If I just add in this date increment algorithm, and alter the step rate by a factor of two. Yeah, I think I may have something for you. Try this," he said, then rattled off another series of characters.

Sydney entered the password as Marshall read it off. She could feel the seconds ticking by, aware of the presence of the security man she had heard in the corridor, each second bringing him a little closer to her.

"Merlin," she said, "where is that security guy?"

"He's on the stairs, Phoenix. Looks like the second floor landing, and moving down. Well below your location."

She knew someone at headquarters would have alerted her had the man come close to entering, but she still breathed a little easier. She focused on the task at hand, staring at the computer screen, willing it to divulge its secrets.

Suddenly a rapid series of images flashed across the monitor, and the Global Oil logo appeared on the screen.

"Merlin, we're in," she said.

In Los Angeles, Marshall executed a series of

commands, sending them remotely now that the system was open to him. He quickly began downloading the customer database and all records of payment, along with production and personnel data. The one piece of information they needed might be hidden somewhere in the mass of information in the files. *I hope we find it, and soon,* Sydney thought as she watched the numbers stream across the screen.

"All set, Phoenix, Outrigger. Now get the hell out of there," Marshall said at last.

"Roger that, Merlin," Dixon said. "Getting the hell out of here, at once."

"The security guy is back on the first floor. You're clear to move," Marshall told the agents.

They left the room and moved back toward the stairwell. But when Sydney opened the door, a piercing siren went off.

"Merlin, this is Outrigger. We've triggered an alarm. What's our best escape route?" Dixon asked calmly.

"Hold on, Outrigger," Marshall replied. "The security guys are headed your way. One's heading for the stairwell, another for the elevators. Once he starts up, you can take the other car—no, wait.

He's locked down the elevators. Your only choice is the stairs."

Sydney could hear heavy footsteps running up the metal treads below them. The only way to go was up, to the roof.

As they ran, Dixon pulled a quick-release hook from his pack. The hook was attached to a shank of high-tensile line. He reached the roof hatch and pushed the door, but it didn't budge. He tried a second time. It was locked.

"Give me a minute, Phoenix," he said.

"You got it," Sydney replied, turning to face the security guard who was rounding the corner on the last flight of stairs. "Just let me know when you're through."

The guard's gun was drawn, but Sydney was expecting him. Grabbing the hand rail, she swung her body around in a sort of cartwheel and kicked the weapon from his hand. The guard hesitated only a fraction of a second. As Sydney kicked off from the wall, he grabbed her left leg, stopping her in mid-arc. She quickly planted her right food and then kicked off again in the reverse direction, bringing the thick rubber sole of her right boot against his temple.

The guard faltered and released her leg. He stumbled back and toppled down the stairs.

On the landing above Sydney, Dixon concentrated on his lock picks, straining to feel and hear the tumblers falling into place. He ignored the fracas behind him, trusting Sydney to do her job and keep the guards at bay.

Back on his feet at the foot of the stairs, the guard pulled a nightstick from his belt and advanced on Sydney. In her ear she could hear her father talking to Dixon.

"Outrigger, this is Raptor. I'm moving to the pickup point. Do you need help?"

"No," Dixon said. "Sounds like Phoenix has it under control." He sighed in relief. "I just got the lock open."

"Good," Sydney said. "Because I've had enough of this guy." She caught the guard's upraised nightstick in both hands, and in one swift move pinned his arm behind his back.

Sydney pushed harder, feeling a sudden give as the guard's shoulder dislocated. He grunted in pain, then fell to his knees.

Dixon was holding the door open. Sydney took the stairs back up two at a time and followed her partner through the door. He swung it closed, but there wasn't time to lock it as they ran for the edge of the building. The alley that separated the Global Oil building from the single-story office building next door was just wide enough to let a truck pass through.

Dixon anchored the line around a sturdy ventilator pipe and expertly threw the hook, clipping it on to a tall ventilation duct that sat on the roof of the adjacent building. Snapping a clip from his harness to the line, he positioned himself on the edge of the roof, and jumped.

Dixon zipped down the line, landing safely on the adjacent roof. Sydney had clipped on and was preparing to jump when two guards burst through the door from the stairs. One carried an automatic weapon, and the second one, holding his dislocated arm at an odd angle, cursed at her. The injured one yelled something to his companion, gesturing that he wanted the gun. Distracted, the guard turned away from Sydney, who took the opportunity to continue making her escape. She went over the side of the building, zipping across the alley and landing on the rooftop below. Dixon quickly unfastened the line, reset the hook, and fed the line over the far side of the building. In a few seconds they were on the ground and running for the pickup location.

"We're on our way, Raptor," Dixon reported.

"Roger that. I'll be waiting," Jack answered.

Minutes later the two agents strolled along a deserted pier in the Lagos Harbor, boarded a waiting boat, and sped away into the night.

Sydney was wide awake. Considering she had just completed back-to-back missions, she should have been sleeping on the flight back to Los Angeles. Instead she sat staring out the window into the pitch-black night, her reflection staring back at her.

Behind her Jack slept soundly. It was a trait she had not inherited from him, and sometimes she envied his ability to sleep whenever, and wherever, the opportunity arose. Early in her career, he had advised her to eat or sleep whenever she could, because an agent never knew when the chance would come again. She tried to follow his advice, but tonight sleep wouldn't come.

Sitting a few seats away, Dixon was also awake. Sydney saw him moving restlessly, as though he couldn't get comfortable. She unfastened her seat belt and rose from her seat. Maybe a little company would do them both good.

"How are you doing?" she asked, slipping into a seat across the aisle from Dixon. "It looks like you can't sleep either."

Dixon glanced at her and then away. "I'm okay," he replied. But there was a distant tone in his voice that discouraged further questions. "I'll just be glad to be home for a few days."

Sydney nodded in agreement. "It will be good to see Nadia, if she isn't back out on assignment," she said. "The last couple of times I've been home, she's been gone."

Dixon shrugged. "That's the job," he said, as though that was all the explanation that was necessary.

Sydney waited, hoping he would say something more. She would have welcomed some conversation, but Dixon was lost in his own thoughts. After a couple minutes of silence she stood up and returned to her seat, but she continued to watch Dixon, wondering what was troubling him.

A few minutes later she saw him take something from the inside pocket of his suit jacket and sit staring at it. From where she was, Sydney could tell it was a photograph, but it took her a moment to identify the people in it. It was Dixon's kids, Steven and Robin.

He stared at the picture for another minute or two, then slid it back into his pocket, turned off the overhead light, and leaned back with a sigh.

CHAPTER 4

APO HEADQUARTERS
LOS ANGELES

Sydney peered over Marshall's shoulder at the data scrolling across his computer screen.

"We've managed to pull out everything in their database, including every transfer of funds for the last eighteen months," he said. "We think a lot of the people they paid are not the kind of people you want to do business with, if you get my drift. But I've searched everything, and I don't find any reference to Blake."

Sydney sighed. She hadn't slept in two days, and she had barely been home in over a week, except to pack a suitcase. "So you're saying we have nothing?"

Marshall turned to look up at her, squinting slightly. "Oh, it's not nothing, if by that you mean we didn't get any information. There is actually quite a lot of information here, including intel about some terrorist activities that seem to be financed by money from the oil operation."

Sydney opened her mouth, but Marshall put up his hand. "I know, I know. You meant we have nothing about Blake. Which we don't, you're right."

Marshall's face fell as he admitted his failure to find the information they wanted. It wasn't his fault—the information wasn't there to find—but Sydney knew how personally he took his job. In addition, this case was personal. He had been kidnapped and held at gunpoint, and he wanted to track down the man who had done it.

Vaughn came into Marshall's gadget-filled workroom. He smiled at Sydney, and she smiled warmly back, welcoming the distraction from her bleak mood. Despite everything, she wanted to give their relationship another chance, and seeing Vaughn's smile always lifted her spirits.

"I just got a message from Langley," he said.

"The intel on the Libyan terrorist cell was very helpful. They are going to take them down tonight. The director wanted to thank us for the tip."

Marshall brightened at the validation of his work. They might not have a lead on Blake, but his work on the database would bring down another terrorist cell. It was the first bit of good news the team had received in days.

"Syd," Vaughn said, turning to Sydney, "I wanted to ask you—"

He was interrupted by Arvin Sloane, who stopped in the doorway. Though his weathered face and gray brush cut showed his age, he still radiated energy. The strength of his presence drew the attention of everyone in the room.

"Vaughn, Sydney, I need you in my office," he said. "Please," he added, as though making a request, not giving an order. Both agents knew better.

They followed Sloane to his stark white office and sat down across the desk from him. Dixon was already there waiting.

On the desk was a stack of files, which Sloane shuffled for a moment before speaking.

"Evan Blake *is* a hijacker and a kidnapper. He

is likely a saboteur. What he *isn't*, is a criminal mastermind." He picked up a file folder, turned it around, and pushed it across the wide desk for Sydney and Vaughn to see.

Dixon sat back, already familiar with the information Sloane was presenting. He appeared calm, completely in control of himself and the situation. This was nothing new. Dixon was a pro.

"If you look at the evaluations," Sloane continued, pointing to specific items in the folder, "you will see that Mr. Blake is very good at his job, but he lacks imagination and initiative. He is long on muscle, as Agent Dixon can attest," he looked at Dixon, who nodded, "but short on brains.

"Basically," Sloane said, "he is ill-suited to plan a sophisticated act of sabotage."

Dixon took over, reaching for another folder. "He lacks the long-term planning skills necessary to pull off something like the sabotage of the drilling platform. He is extremely knowledgeable, judging from his work history. But he's not an instigator. Blake is not the type to plan a long-range campaign of sabotage."

Sloane opened a final folder and glanced over the information inside. "The assessment of Mr.

Blake's abilities became critical this morning, when I received a classified piece of intel. It appears that there has recently been a failure at a refinery in Omsk. Of course, the Russians aren't admitting anything." He passed a reconnaissance photo across the desk. Vaughn took it, holding it so that both he and Sydney could see it.

Dixon spoke up. "We think it is more than a coincidence that there has been trouble at two different oil facilities within a matter of days. We believe there may be a single source for the problems. Blake isn't capable of planning such a campaign; therefore, he's working for someone else. We need to find out who that is."

Sloane gestured to the photographs spread across his desk. "The Russians may once again be covering up an industrial and environmental disaster. We have no way of knowing how bad it is, without firsthand information, and they are not about to give it to us. In addition, you will look for any link to Blake, or his employer. The three of you will leave for Omsk in two hours. Your primary task is to assess the damage to the plant, and the potential harm to the local and global environment. Remember Chernobyl—the damage went well beyond their borders, without advance warning. We don't want another incident like that one. Now, if there are no questions . . ." He looked expectantly from one face to the next.

Sydney rose to her feet.

She would sleep on the plane.

OMSK REFINERY
OMSK, SIBERIA

The parking lot outside the refinery was covered in a light dusting of snow. Sydney and Vaughn walked between the collection of utilitarian sedans, leaving a trail of footprints in their wake.

Sydney adjusted her earpiece. "Can you hear me, Merlin?"

"Loud and clear, Phoenix," came Marshall's reply. "Got you on the uplink. How about you, Outrigger?"

"Got you both," Dixon said from his position a few blocks away. "You're clear to proceed anytime."

"Ready?" Sydney asked as she looked over at Vaughn. He was in white coveralls, dressed as a member of the engineering crew that was currently swarming to the refinery to deal with whatever it was the Russians were trying to cover up. Sydney was dressed in a plain gray pleated skirt, a non-descript white blouse, a beige button-down sweater, and sensible brown shoes, the standard uniform of refinery middle management.

Vaughn nodded. "Shotgun and Phoenix are in play," he said as they approached the main entrance to the facility.

Sydney and Vaughn separated in the building lobby. Vaughn ran a magnetic key card through a reader, and passed through an unmarked heavy steel door on his way to access the extent of the damage to the plant. Sydney watched until he was through the door, then turned and started walking in the opposite direction, determined to find a link to Blake.

As she passed down the unsecured corridor, Sydney allowed herself a moment of amazement. The open offices she passed were filled with filing cabinets with towers of papers sitting on top of them, as though waiting to be filed. She couldn't remember the last time she had seen that many paper files in such disarray.

"I would say that confirms the rumors about the delays in converting to electronic filing," Dixon said as he watched the images from the miniature camera hidden in a button of Sydney's sweater.

"I agree, Outrigger," Sydney said as she ducked into an empty office and glanced over the sheets of paper at the top of the stack. "These files don't look like anything useful. But I wouldn't expect to find what we're looking for in an unsecured location."

"Roger that, Phoenix," Marshall said, scanning the images as they appeared at his lab at APO headquarters. "They look like some kind of vending machine logs. Looks like the employees are mighty fond of something called chocolate cheese rings, if I'm not mistaken. That sounds pretty awful. But you're right. This isn't what we're looking for."

"Roger, Merlin. But I can use these files as props," Sydney said. She gathered up a handful of papers and continued down the hall. A few yards farther down she came to another door. On the frosted window were flaking Cyrillic characters that told her this was the personnel files room.

She pushed open the door. The reception room was cramped, stuffed with three orange plastic chairs, a typing table, and a cheap desk with a scarred plastic top.

A young receptionist, who might have been pretty if her skin hadn't been so sallow and permanently chapped from the cold, sat at the desk, guarding the door to the file area with a scowl on her face.

"Hello," Sydney greeted her in Russian.

"Can I help you?" the girl asked in a voice that indicated she had no intention of helping Sydney, if she could avoid it.

"I just have these records." Sydney indicated the stack of papers cradled against her chest. "They have to go back in the files."

The girl's scowl deepened as she glanced at an overflowing tray of papers on her desk. "They all have to go back into the files," she said. She sounded tired and her shoulders sagged as she spoke, as though the weight of the filing was more than she could bear.

This was what Sydney had hoped for. "I have a few minutes," she said, warmth flowing in her voice. "Why don't I put these away myself? It isn't as though you don't have enough to do."

The girl's face brightened for a moment, then the scowl returned. "I am not supposed to let anyone into the file room without proper authorization."

"Well," Sydney said, lowering her voice to a conspiratorial whisper, "I won't tell anyone if you won't."

The girl's contempt for filing overcame her desire to fulfill her guard duties. "Okay," she said, "but don't remove anything."

"I won't," Sydney assured her, and she passed through the door into the file room. She tugged the door behind her so that it was nearly closed but didn't appear to have been deliberately shut.

She looked around the small room. Every wall was lined with file cabinets, most of them with stacks of paper on top, waiting to be put away.

"Shotgun," she said, softly, "I'm in position. Do you have any names for me?"

From the other end of the facility Michael Vaughn answered. "I've only had time to check a few maintenance logs. There are a couple so far that might fit based on their dates of employment: Ilya Golovina and Leon Nosova. Give me a minute, and I should have some more."

Sydney scanned the drawer labels, located the proper drawer, and took out the file on Ilya Golovina. She aimed the button of her coat at the pages of data and scanned quickly through the stacks. Then she repeated the process with the Nosova file.

She read the pages as she transmitted the images back to Marshall, her heart sinking. Both of the men had clean records and sterling evaluations; even their attendance was exemplary. She knew already that neither of them was the man they were seeking.

She replaced the files, tucking a few of her decoy pages into the back of one of the drawers. It wouldn't be to her benefit to have someone find them sitting out and wonder how they got there. Judging by the general lack of organization, she suspected no one would ever see them where she had stashed them.

She continued to check three more files as Vaughn supplied names, with no more success.

From his post Dixon spoke. "Phoenix, Shotgun, this is Outrigger. You have five minutes until the shift change. Be ready to move when you hear the whistle."

"Shotgun, do you have anything else?" Sydney asked hurriedly.

"Try Ivan Bazhukov. He's mentioned in one of the reports," he said, then added very quietly, "Gotta go, someone's coming."

Sydney stuffed the rest of her prop pages into the back of a crowded file drawer, and then pulled out the file on Bazhukov. She flipped the file open and stared at his employee identification photo. Glaring back at her from the grainy photo was the man she knew as Evan Blake.

"We've got him," she said. She pulled the pages from the file, transmitting the images to Marshall at APO headquarters. There were several pages of medical records, indicating Bazhukov had been on leave for the past few days due to an injury. *And I bet the dates of his leave coincide with his employment at Petroleum Associates,* Sydney thought.

"Phoenix," Vaughn's voice sounded in her ear. "I'm almost to the lobby. Are you clear?"

"Not yet," she replied. "I just have a couple more pages to scan. You go ahead. I'll meet you at the pickup spot in five minutes."

She was scanning the last page when the door opened behind her. "It's quitting time," the young woman said in a bland tone. "Leave the rest of that for the next shift."

"Got it, Phoenix," Marshall said in Syd's ear.

Sydney closed the folder and replaced it in the

drawer before turning around. "You are so kind to remind me," she said. "But I just finished, so we don't have to leave anything." She walked to the door and followed the girl through the cramped outer chamber and into the hallway.

The girl merely nodded, then locked the door behind them.

Sydney walked briskly down the corridor and through the lobby. Her ramrod-straight posture and determined stride discouraged anyone who might consider exchanging small talk during the crush that was the shift change.

Outside, she turned away from the crowded bus stop where the majority of the employees were headed. Instead she walked with a small knot of workers through the dusk toward the main road. She ducked quickly down a side street, and a block later she was alone. She turned another corner, the buildings shielding her from casual observation. Halfway down the block a battered van idled at the curb. Its dark paint was dull, and spots of rust attested to years of being pelted by snow and rock salt. The only unblemished parts of the vehicle were its tinted windows.

Sydney half-ran the last few yards to the van, anxious to be out of the vicinity of the refinery now that the job was over. Vaughn slid open the side door as she approached, and reached out his hand, pulling her into the van. Then he reached around her to slide the door closed, enveloping her in a half-hug. Dixon put the van in gear and drove away from the refinery toward the outskirts of town. There was a safe house just a few miles away, where they could plan their next move.

Dixon pulled into the parking lot of a nondescript apartment building that sat in the center of a dozen or more identical buildings. The cars in the lot were mostly older, inexpensive models. The van, with its peeling paint and dented fenders, blended right in.

Carrying their equipment in battered suitcases, the three agents entered a tiny elevator in one of the buildings, and Dixon pushed the button for the twelfth floor. They rode up in silence, without even a floor indicator to stare at.

Finally the car slowed, and the button for the twelfth floor popped out with a loud click. The sudden noise jarred Sydney from her thoughts, and she jumped a little.

Dixon chuckled quietly, and said in English, "I always forget that too." Then he reverted to Russian as the doors opened. "At the end of the hall," he said.

The apartment at the end of the hall was blocked by a locked metal grate. Dixon took a key from his pocket, unlocked the grate, let Syd and Vaughn pass through before him, and then locked the grate behind them.

The apartment itself was small but clean. Most of the space was taken up by a central room dominated by a conference table that was surrounded by chairs.

They immediately established a link to headquarters and set to work printing out copies of everything that had been scanned from Bazhukov's personnel file. Although Sydney and Dixon had seen it as it uploaded, this was Vaughn's first look at the picture of the man they were persuing.

"I only got a glimpse of him from the air," he said, "but this is the guy. I'm sure of it."

"Me too," said Sydney.

Dixon nodded, tight-lipped. This was the man he had fought with, the man who had kidnapped Marshall because Dixon had failed to stop him.

Dixon pointed to the attendance records, showing the dates that Bazhukov had been on disability leave. "He didn't seem disabled the last time I saw him," Dixon muttered. "Look, there's a local address in the file. Why don't we go see if he's home, maybe have a little chat with Mr. Bazhukov, ask him what he was doing in the Gulf of Mexico?"

"Affirmative, Outrigger." It was Arvin Sloane, speaking from Los Angeles. "We'd like you to invite Mr. Bazhukov back to L.A. for a little chat, if you would."

Sloane's suave tone did nothing to hide his real intent. They needed to interrogate Bazhukov, preferably at APO headquarters, to find out what he knew.

Thirty minutes later Syd, Vaughn, and Dixon were back in the van, following Marshall's directions. But when they reached the address, they knew they were too late. The address for Bazhukov was a burned-out building in a block of abandoned apartment buildings. Sagging chain-link fencing surrounded the derelict structures, and rusting metal signs indicated that the entire block was set for demolition.

It was yet another dead end.

CHAPTER 5

Sydney climbed wearily aboard the transport plane and settled into one of the wide seats. Vaughn stopped next to her in the aisle. He looked as haggard as she felt—they were both exhausted from the back-to-back assignments. They both understood that it was better if they kept their distance. For right now Sydney didn't want to talk to him, or think about where their relationship had been and where it was going. She just wanted to rest.

Vaughn gave her a weary smile, walked past her, dropped into a seat a few feet away, and strapped himself in. He was silent as they took off, and he didn't move once they were in the air.

A few minutes after they had reached their cruising altitude, Sydney risked a quick glance in his direction. His eyes were closed, and his chest rose and fell slowly. Deep lines of fatigue and worry were etched into his face, even in his sleep.

Sydney wished she could fall asleep. She ached with exhaustion, but she couldn't shut down, couldn't let herself relax. She felt as though she were chasing a ghost. Every time they got close to the man she still thought of as Blake, he slipped away. He had eluded her on the oil platform, his picture had mocked her from the file in Omsk, and the burned-out apartment had been a final slap.

Where is he? Who is he working for? she wondered, frustrated.

A few feet away she saw Marcus Dixon shift in his seat. Maybe she could talk to him about the mission. Rehashing the details might help them see something they'd missed earlier.

She unfastened her seat belt and stood up. She admired Dixon, his strength and his calm. He somehow managed to balance his personal life and the demands of the job, even after the tragic death of his wife. Sometimes she felt she looked up to him more than she did to her own father.

Sydney slid into a seat facing Dixon, watching the lines of worry vanish from his face as he hid his concerns from her.

"What's on your mind, Sydney?"

"I was about to ask you the same thing. I wanted to talk about the mission, but it looks like you're already deep in thought."

Dixon shifted in his seat. His eyes met hers briefly, then his gaze slid away.

"It was nothing."

"Dixon," Sydney said. She reached out and touched his hand. She considered him a friend as well as a colleague, and she wanted to help him if she could. "It looks like more than 'nothing.'"

He waved off her concern. "Really, it isn't important."

"You know," Sydney went ahead, "it feels like we just had this same conversation, on the flight home from our last mission."

Dixon shook his head, as though trying to deny it, but she knew better. It *was* the same conversation, and Dixon had the same look on his face, whatever the cause.

She recalled seeing him looking at the photograph of Robin and Steven that he'd carried with him on their last trip.

"Is it the kids?" she asked, her voice gentle. "Is there something wrong at home?"

Robin and Steven were the center of Dixon's life. When they had been taken a couple of years earlier, it had nearly destroyed him, and their return had been a relief for everyone. Without them he would have been lost.

"The kids are fine, Sydney. They screw up sometimes, just like regular kids, but they're fine."

"Then, what is it?"

Dixon sighed. "You aren't going to let this drop, are you?"

Sydney squeezed his hand, then let it go and sat back. "Not a chance." She grinned, knowing he would tell her. "And you'd pester me if you knew something was bothering me, so don't even try to back out of it."

Dixon smiled faintly, but the worry remained in his eyes. "It's Marshall," he said.

"Marshall?" She stared at him for a moment, trying to figure out what he meant. "Has he done something?"

"No," Dixon drew the single syllable out, stalling. But he knew Sydney wouldn't quit until he gave her an explanation. Outside the plane, the sky was black. Inside, the dim lights created an intimate atmosphere, one that invited confidences. "It's not anything *he* did. It's what *I* did."

"You didn't do anything to Marshall," she said.

"Maybe not this time, but I came close. I nearly got him killed, because I didn't stop Blake." Dixon paused for a moment. "It made me think about what the team would be like without him. Marshall is an invaluable resource, and I would hate to lose him," Dixon continued.

"You could say that about any of us," Sydney countered. "Every member of this team—you, Vaughn, my father, Nadia, Weiss, even Sloane— we're all valuable assets. We all have skills and strengths that contribute to the team's ability to take down the bad guys."

She waved a hand to stop his protest, as though she could anticipate what he was about to say. "I know Marshall is a technical wizard, one of the best in the business—in the world. And we are lucky to have him. But what makes him different from anyone else?"

Dixon just looked at her, then turned toward the window. He sat in silence for a couple of minutes, staring at the inky blackness that filled the night sky.

Sydney waited, not willing to end the conversation. There was more to Dixon's worries than Marshall's technical skills, or his encyclopedic knowledge of obscure information. She wanted an explanation, and she was prepared to wait him out.

Finally, Dixon turned back to her, his face an impassive mask. "It's tough to put your life on the line, Sydney, no matter who you are or what you're doing. And we do just that every time we go out in the field." He sat forward and the mask cracked, betraying an intensity in his expression that underscored his words. "It's even tougher when you know there are people at home who are depending on you. People like Carrie and Mitchell, who depend on Marshall to come home to them. Children need both their parents, Sydney. You know that."

Sydney winced as she thought of her mother, who had abandoned her to return to the Soviet Union when her cover was blown—the woman who had left her with a distant and grieving father. "Yes, I probably understand that better than most people," she finally admitted. Then she looked hard at Dixon. "But is it really Mitchell you're thinking about, or is it Steven and Robin? They need their parent too."

Dixon raised a hand in surrender and smiled tentatively.

"You don't quit, do you, Syd? You're right, I do worry about Steven and Robin. I wonder what would happen to them if I wasn't around." He sat up straight again and stuck his chin out. "I just have to believe I'll come home, every time, after every mission. I hang on to that belief. I have to."

SYDNEY'S HOME
LOS ANGELES

It was still dark when Sydney got home. She fumbled with her key, finally got the door unlocked, and then stepped into the quiet house.

Inside, a single lamp burned in the living room, providing enough illumination for her to see that there was someone lying on the sofa.

Nadia was home.

The noise of the door opening had roused her sister, who sat up as Sydney crossed the room. Nadia pushed her dark hair back from her face and squinted sleepily at Sydney.

"Hi there," Sydney said, dropping onto the sofa and hugging Nadia, glad to see her half sister. Sydney had been raised as an only child, and hadn't known of Nadia's existence until she had been discovered in connection with the Rambaldi investigation a couple of years earlier. "If you were waiting up for me, you weren't doing a very good job," she teased.

It felt good to have someone to wait up for her, even if Nadia had fallen asleep.

"Eric was here for a while. We thought you might get in earlier," Nadia said. She gestured toward the kitchen, nearly invisible in the darkened house. "There are leftovers in the refrigerator, if you're hungry. Would you like me to fix you a plate?"

"I ate on the plane, but thanks anyway," Sydney said. She stood up. "How was your trip?"

"Long. Tiring. At least we found the man that was missing," Nadia said, assuming correctly that Sydney knew about her mission.

"That's good. You were looking for a rocket scientist who had disappeared, right?" Sydney asked. She went into her room, pulled off her travel clothes, and grabbed an oversize T-shirt from her dresser. "What happened?" She asked as she returned to the living room.

Nadia was sitting up, the blanket drawn around her shoulders, when Sydney walked back into the room. "Turns out, he had taken a little vacation, without bothering to tell his superiors. Something to do with an office romance he didn't want anyone to know about."

Sydney sat on the other sofa, tucking her legs under her. "Didn't Sloane think the woman involved was a terrorist?"

Nadia's chuckle was soft and quiet. "My father thinks everyone is as devious as he is. I don't think it ever occurred to him that the man was just trying to be discreet," she said.

Sydney sighed. "Discreet, secretive, what's the difference? After all the years we've been doing this, how can we not be suspicious?"

"I don't think my father knows anymore what it is like to be a regular person. To him everything has a double or triple meaning," Nadia said, then yawned. "How about you? How was your trip?"

Sydney gave Nadia a brief summary of her mission. There wasn't much to tell; they had found Blake's trail, but he had been a step ahead of them once again. "You said Eric was here, right? How's his shoulder?" Sydney asked suddenly.

"It is okay. The bruise is healed," Nadia said. She shrugged. "It's part of the job."

Nadia was right; it was part of the job. But Sydney couldn't help frowning. Her conversation with Dixon was still bothering her. It wasn't just the agents who took risks, it was their loved ones, too.

The two sisters continued to talk quietly as they drifted toward sleep.

Nadia fell back asleep, and Sydney sat in the darkened room, listening to her sister's steady breathing. She wondered if she would ever be able to have a normal life. *I can hope,* she thought, then finally relaxed and felt sleep take hold.

APO HEADQUARTERS
LOS ANGELES

Marcus Dixon rode through the tunnels of the Los Angeles subway system, exited the train, and walked to the far end of the line once the station was empty.

He waited, making sure he was alone, before executing the complicated series of maneuvers that opened a hidden door. He walked down a tunnel and through a security checkpoint, eventually reaching the underground headquarters of APO.

The contrast between the dark subway tunnels and the APO offices, which were stark white and flooded with artificial light, was startling. It was hard to believe the entire complex was hundreds of feet below Los Angeles.

He glanced around the spacious room as he settled at his desk and took a stack of file folders from his drawer. He looked back through the accumulated intelligence they had gathered on Blake. If he just kept looking, he was sure he could find a clue, some piece of information that would allow them to find the elusive criminal. Dixon was deep into the dossier, comparing notes between the personnel files from Petroleum Associates and Omsk, looking for something that would lead them to the man who had attacked him and kidnapped Marshall, when his phone rang.

It was an outside call to his direct line, a number that very few people knew. He stopped reading and dropped into his cover role.

"Marcus Dixon," he answered on the second ring. "How may I help you?"

"Mr. Dixon? This is Charlotte Reynolds, Steven's principal. Do you have a moment?"

Dixon's heart was in his throat. The last time he had received a call like this, Steven and Robin had been abducted. He swallowed hard, pushing aside the memory.

"Certainly, Ms. Reynolds."

"Mr. Dixon, I know you are a concerned and involved parent, and Steven is a good child. But he was involved in another altercation at school this morning."

"*Another* altercation?"

There was an embarrassed silence from the other end of the phone. After a moment Ms. Reynolds answered, "I believe Mrs. Sutton, Steven's teacher, discussed his behavior with you a few weeks ago?"

Dixon closed his eyes and stifled a groan. Steven's teacher had mentioned something, but he had talked to Steven, and he thought the problem had been resolved. Apparently, he was wrong.

"Yes, she did mention it, and I did talk to Steven. It sounds as if the situation has not improved."

"Well," the principal began, "it did get better

for a while. But Steven has been involved in two scuffles in the past week."

Dixon shook his head. "I'll talk to him again, Ms. Reynolds. You have my word, this is not considered acceptable behavior in our house, and Steven's attitude will improve."

"I appreciate that, Mr. Dixon. And I know you are doing your best. But will you allow me to make a suggestion?" She hesitated again, and Dixon bit back the impulse to tell her to get on with it. Instead he murmured his assent.

"Mr. Dixon, have you considered getting some help for Steven?" she asked. "He's not a seriously troubled child," she continued hastily. "But sometimes, especially with children, the mourning process is short-circuited, only to be triggered by a stressful event later on. The transition to high school is a difficult one for any child, and Steven may be reacting to that stress. I know it has been some time since Steven's mother died, but her death may be part of why he is acting out now."

Dixon heard a quiet cough behind him, and he turned to see Marshall standing next to his desk. How long had he been there? Had he heard any of Dixon's conversation? Dixon held up a finger, gesturing for Marshall to wait while he ended the call.

"I understand your concern, Ms. Reynolds, and I will consider your suggestion. Perhaps I can call you in a day or two, and we can discuss this in more detail?"

"Of course. I know you will need some time to address the issue at home, Mr. Dixon, and I am sorry to have to disturb you at work," the principal replied.

Dixon hung up the phone, and then looked up at Marshall.

Marshall raised his dark eyebrows. "Problem?"

"Kids. Well, kid," Dixon said, then waved the subject away. "Not anything to worry about, just typical teenager stuff," he lied. "What can I do for you?"

"Well, I just wanted to tell you, I took another look at those pictures you guys brought back from Siberia. That's definitely the guy that hijacked the helicopter. Well, he didn't so much hijack it as steal it, since there wasn't a pilot in it at the time. Yeah, more like steal," Marshall rambled.

Dixon kept his face impassive, but he felt a shadow of guilt pass over him. It wasn't an emotion an agent should be plagued with, so he pushed it away. The helicopter incident had happened days ago; there was nothing more he could do. It was time to forget it and move on.

"But I did get a good look at him after we were in the air, since there wasn't much of anything else to do, what with him flying. And I can say that was definitely him."

Marshall paused for breath.

"I was sure it was," Dixon cut in.

"It's not just what I saw, either," Marshall went on. "I got some pictures of him, when he wasn't watching me, and we analyzed them against the Omsk personnel photo. He's definitely the same guy. The distance between the eyes is exactly twenty-eight millimeters, and the jawline matches, and—"

Dixon stood up, interrupting the endless flow of words. "Thanks, Marshall."

"You're welcome," Marshall said.

Dixon waited for Marshall to walk away, but instead he hovered by the desk, as though there was something else on his mind.

"Something's bothering you," Marshall said, resting his hip against the edge of Dixon's desk. He looked as though he was settling in, and wasn't going to be dissuaded by Dixon's attempts to terminate the conversation. "What is it? You can talk to me about it, if you want. Now that I have Mitchell, I know what it's like to be a father," he said.

Dixon wondered if *everyone* was going to get on him about the kids. First Sydney, and now Marshall. How many times could he brush off their questions?

Marshall continued to look at him, clearly expecting an answer. Dixon sighed. He didn't see any alternative but to answer Marshall's question.

"Steven's in trouble at school. Getting in fights, cutting class. Stuff he knows I won't tolerate."

Marshall winced. "That's too bad. But maybe somebody's bothering him, like a bully or something. Maybe he had to defend himself. . . ." Marshall's voice trailed off, and he looked down at his feet, as though he might have revealed more than he'd intended.

"Could be, I suppose," Dixon said. "But that's no excuse. You try to protect your kids, to be there when they need you, but it's tough. It's hard to give them the time and energy they require." He looked at his desk, which was covered with files, then glanced around the office full of agents, all working on cases that could decide the fate of nations. "We do important work here. But sometimes it gets in the way of family obligations." He looked back at Marshall, his eyes hard. "You understand that, don't you? How it can get in the way?"

Marshall nodded, then looked over Dixon's shoulder. He tilted his head slightly in that direction.

Dixon turned to find Jack standing behind him, his face a blank mask.

"Sloane wants us all in the conference room. He's got some information," Jack announced.

The agents filed into the sleek glass conference room and took their places around the table. Dixon glanced up at Jack once or twice as they were settling in, unsure of how much Jack had overheard, but Jack made no acknowledgment of the conversation.

Sydney sat between Dixon and Vaughn. The three agents had been in the field together on the last task, and they were painfully aware of the lack of progress.

Marshall and Jack sat down facing the three field agents.

Arvin Sloane paced around the table, like a

small caged animal. He was almost constantly in motion, as though unwilling, or unable, to stop.

Like a shark, Dixon thought.

"We have some hard information, some conjectures, and some rumors," Sloane said by way of introduction. He circled the table again, gesturing to the files in front of each of the agents. "The logs Mr. Vaughn retrieved from Omsk clearly indicate damage to equipment there. Damage which, though slight, does not appear to be normal wear and tear."

Sloane then pointed a remote control at a projector, and Bazhukov's face appeared on the wall-mounted screen, alongside a photograph of Blake. "As you can see, these men are one and the same. Mr. Flinkman has analyzed the facial structure, and Agent Vaughn has made a comparison of leave records."

Vaughn sat forward, leaning his arms on the tabletop. He looked around the table, then back at his notes. He cleared his throat and addressed the room. "We were able to make a correlation between the dates of Bazhukov's medical leave and the dates of Blake's employment with Petroleum Associates. Based on those records, we can see that this plan has been under way for at least a month. We feel confident that this conjecture is correct."

"But Blake was only with Petroleum Associates for the last week or so, right?" Sydney asked. She looked at her file, confirming what she remembered from her interview with Jack Clark, the oil platform engineer.

"True," Vaughn replied. "But when he went to work there, he listed references from a large oil cartel in the Middle East. Apparently, he worked there in the interim. And the man who controls that cartel is Cristos Soukis."

Sloane pressed a button on the remote control, and another face appeared on the screen. The dark, hooded eyes burned with intensity, even in a grainy, long-lens photo.

Vaughn continued. "Soukis owns one of the largest, and most profitable, shipping companies in Greece. He is reported to be worth at least three billion dollars."

Sloane cut in. "The source of his fortune is supposed to be his shipping activities, but we suspect he has other resources, if you will. This is also conjecture, backed by observation. But Soukis has never been charged with a crime, and, given his wealth, probably never will be. We believe Blake was recruited and put in place by Soukis—through a subordinate, of course. The letters of recommendation carry authentic signatures."

"Why would Soukis want to damage the oil operations?" Jack asked. "If he makes money shipping oil, wouldn't he want the fields to be producing at full capacity?"

"Soukis has much more interest in oil than just hauling it around the world," Sloane answered. "He has a reputation as a speculator, and he has been placing orders for oil shares through a series of intermediaries and subsidiaries. He's tried to cover his tracks, but with a market tracking program developed by Mr. Flinkman, we have been able to follow his spending around the globe. This is confirmed intel."

"Right," Marshall said. He tapped out a series of keystrokes on his laptop, and a complex chart replaced Soukis's picture on the projection screen.

"You see this red line here?" Marshall pointed at the chart. "That represents Soukis's annual purchases of oil shares for the last five years. As you can see, the slope is very small. Not much change."

He tapped again, and the chart zoomed in on the last quarter of the time line. "But if you look at the last year, you can see a sudden upswing in the past few months. When you take into account the fluctuations of the oil market and superimpose the overall market trends . . . ," he said, tapping on the keyboard. A blue line appeared, paralleling the red one, then diverging widely in the recent months. "You can see this is unusual behavior for Soukis. And—" He started to tap again, but Sloane cut him off.

"As I said, Mr. Flinkman's analysis gives us a strong indication that Soukis is demonstrating an unusual buying pattern. So far we have some solid assumptions, backed by intelligence that seems to support our position."

Sloane stopped pacing for a minute, and Sydney watched him in anticipation. Whether she liked the man or not, she had to admit he could captivate everyone in the room with the force of his personality. He was the man in control.

Sydney wondered if he derived some kind of enjoyment from making them wait. She suspected he did.

"Now comes the rumor," Sloane said at last. He

started pacing again. "We've heard from a couple of well-placed sources that Soukis still has buy orders going out, but only for the next seventy-two hours. After that all of his representatives have been instructed to stop buying, and to hold all shares until further notice. Cristos Soukis is going to execute his plan within the next three days. And it is up to us to find out what that plan is, and stop it." He paused in front of the screen, which he had switched back to the picture of Soukis. "We need to determine what Soukis has to gain from the destruction of oil production capacity, and how to thwart his plan. I want updates every two hours, starting now."

He glanced at the face scowling out at all of them from the screen, then back at the assembled team. He pointed at Soukis. "We have three days to stop this man."

CHAPTER 6

"Jack?" Sloane's voice stopped Jack in his tracks as he followed the rest of the team out of the conference room. "May I have a moment?" Sloane asked, then gestured down the hall. "My office, if you don't mind."

The two men walked in silence to Sloane's office, and Sloane closed the door behind them. Jack knew the others would be watching through the glass walls, wondering what else Sloane might have to say about the Soukis situation.

Sloane walked behind his glass and chrome

desk and turned to face Jack. "We need Bazhukov."

"Yes, we do," Bristow agreed. "But knowing we need him and having him are two different things. And he has proven to be a rather elusive target."

Sloane nodded as he sat down. "I have already reached out to some of my old contacts," he said. "No one has heard of him. He appears to have no record, no history of criminal behavior. Nothing. As far as anyone knows, he's nothing more than a thin stack of papers in a file somewhere."

"Tell that to Dixon," Jack said sarcastically.

Sloane nodded. Leaning forward in his chair, he rested his elbows on the edge of his desk. "Exactly. He exists, we just don't know where he is."

"I have a few more people I could ask," Jack said. "I once worked with an oil executive. A kidnap threat. It might be time to call in the favor."

"Do that, Jack. Let me know what you find," Sloane said.

"I will," Jack said. He rose from the chair where he'd been sitting and crossed the room. At the door he looked back at Sloane. It seemed odd that the man had called him in privately for this exchange. "Was there something else?"

Sloane hesitated, then shook his head. "No,"

he said. "Just let me know what you find out."

Sloane looked down at the papers on his desk and started shuffling through them. The dismissal was obvious. Whatever Sloane had intended to talk to Jack about, he had changed his mind.

Leaving Sloane's office, Jack hesitated as he passed Dixon's desk. He thought about Dixon's kids and what he had overheard, but he kept walking. If Dixon wanted to talk, he would let Jack know. In the meantime they both had work to do.

His call to the oilman contact was warmly received, but the man wasn't optimistic about his chances of finding Blake. "The men I know, we never see the crews. I'll pass the picture around, but to tell the truth it'll probably just end up turned over to some clerk in human resources and never seen again."

Jack thanked him for his time and promised to fax over a copy of Blake's picture. But the oilman's pessimism was contagious.

Time was running out, and Jack needed to find a real lead.

Hours passed without a change. Each member of the team scoured files, hacked into databases, and did anything and everything to try to track down Blake and investigate Cristos Soukis.

Scenarios had been proposed and discarded. Sydney had wanted to go after Soukis directly, but Sloane had vetoed the idea.

"The man is too slick," he said. "He has more security than many small nations, and a lot less restraint." He shook his head. "I don't think we could gain anything by confronting Soukis, and even a covert operation might alert him to our suspicions."

Sydney could feel the tension in the room. Occasionally a phone would ring, and each of them would look expectantly at the recipient of the call until the person on the phone would shake his or her head. No news. Then they would all go back to their search.

Finally, Vaughn caught a break.

Sydney was working her way through a list of contacts in Greece, developing a background profile on Soukis, when she felt a change in the room. It was as though a current had passed through.

She looked up and saw Vaughn on the telephone. He was sitting a little taller, scribbling furiously.

For a minute no one spoke. Vaughn was still on

the phone, writing notes and murmuring encouragingly to his source. No one dared to interrupt, for fear of breaking the flow of information. By the time Vaughn hung up the phone, Sydney felt as though she had been holding her breath for days.

Vaughn stood up, grabbed his notes, and headed for the conference room, beckoning for his fellow agents to join him.

Sloane emerged from his office and joined them in the conference room. "You have something for us, Agent Vaughn?"

Vaughn nodded grimly. "We know where Bazhukov is, but the news isn't as good as I had hoped."

"Indeed?" Sloane arched one eyebrow and crossed his arms over his chest, waiting for the rest of Vaughn's intel.

"Bazhukov was apprehended while trying to leave Siberia. The Russian authorities captured him in Rostov, near the Black Sea. They think he was trying to reach Greece, via Turkey."

"That's the good news, right?" Dixon said. "We know where he is. So what's the bad news?"

Vaughn shook his head. "Bazhukov is being charged with sabotage in connection with the damage to the refinery at Omsk. Apparently his stupidity finally caught up with him. The Russian authorities are taking a hard line against saboteurs. My informant tells me he will be tried immediately, and he will be sentenced to a maximum security facility."

"That is unfortunate." Sloane slid easily into the position of control. "If he is placed in such a facility, he may well be beyond our grasp. We are not going to allow that to happen."

CHAPTER 7

HIGHWAY BETWEEN MOSCOW AND ROSTOV
22 MILES NORTHEAST OF ROSTOV

Sydney crouched behind an overturned sedan at the side of a deserted highway. Early morning light stretched shadows across the gently waving sea of feather grass that covered the steppe. A few yards up the road, Dixon waited, hidden in the grass.

Sydney strained her ears to listen for an approaching vehicle. According to the intel her father had received, a van carrying Bazhukov to Moscow should pass her in a matter of minutes. For a while the only sound was the faint sighing of the breeze through the tall grass. Then, in the distance, she heard the rumble of a diesel engine.

"Get ready, Phoenix," Eric Weiss said, speaking from his vantage point a half mile away. "They're coming your way."

"Affirmative, Houdini. I hear them," Sydney said. She waited a few seconds, dropped a lit match on the pile of dry grass hidden behind the car, then slowly stumbled toward the road. Her blouse was torn and her skirt was ripped, exposing the full length of her long leg. Her feet were bare, her face scratched, and she looked the part of an accident victim.

Sydney stumbled into the narrow road in front of the oncoming van. Unless the driver was willing to run her over, his only choice was to stop.

As the van screeched to a halt, Sydney collapsed on the road. Two uniformed men jumped from the front seat of the van, running to her aid and leaving their prisoner unattended in the back of the vehicle.

"They're both out of the van," Sydney whispered into her comm.

"Roger that, Phoenix," Dixon said. He raised his head to peer over the grass at the guards.

Sydney groaned and moved slightly, letting her

skirt ride higher on her hip. She reached out toward the two men. They were definitely distracted.

"Help me, please," she said in Russian. "I do not know what happened, but the car . . ." She motioned toward the overturned vehicle. Wisps of smoke were curling up from behind it.

"There is a fire extinguisher in the van," the younger of the two guards said, and he turned back to get it.

The older man offered his hand to Sydney, to help her up. She reached up and took his hand, deliberately pulling him toward her and putting him off balance. Glancing behind him, she saw the younger guard climb into the vehicle. He disappeared underneath the dash, probably unhooking the extinguisher from its compartment.

Sydney hoped Dixon was in place behind the van as she sprang to her feet, then she flipped the guard to the ground and onto his back in the middle of the road. He quickly staggered to his feet. He was more agile than Sydney had expected, but the blow had knocked the wind out of him and he struggled to get a deep breath. She didn't give him the chance. She planted one bare foot firmly on the road and kicked the guard in the stomach. The guard doubled over, clutching his midsection. He reached for his gun and fumbled with the snap on his holster. Sydney lunged at him, grabbing his arm and twisting, forcing his hand away from the holster. Then she reversed her force, pulling the guard past her and sending him into the pavement once again.

Sydney heard a shout from the direction of the van, but she couldn't stop to look. Dixon could take care of himself.

Sydney straddled the guard on the ground. She ripped his gun from its holster and flung it into the tall grass. Then she grabbed his left arm and pulled it behind his back.

The guard rolled left, scissoring his legs, trying to knock her legs from under her.

Sydney heard another shout from the direction of the van. The guard glanced away, distracted by the noise, and Sydney took advantage of the opening, landing a solid punch to the side of his head, knocking him out cold. She pulled away a strip of her artfully torn skirt and used it to lash his hands together behind his back, then left him lying in the road while she went to help Dixon.

Sydney sprinted toward the van. Dixon had his gun out, pointed at the driver's side window.

Through the window she could see the young guard, his face pasty. The younger guard had locked himself in the van as soon as he'd realized they were under attack. She saw that he was only a teenager, not much older than Dixon's own children. He looked as though he belonged in school, not ferrying prisoners around the country.

Dixon was talking to the boy, who was shaking with fear. Sydney could see the boy slowly begin to relax. His shoulders lowered a fraction of an inch. Dixon was talking him out of the van.

Sydney took a deep breath. If Dixon could talk the boy out, all the better. She didn't want to fight with a kid, and she knew Dixon wouldn't want to either.

As Sydney watched, the boy placed his hands on the steering wheel. If he had a gun, he was making no move to draw it. A little color had returned to his baby face, making him appear even younger.

The van rocked slightly on its suspension, as though the load inside had shifted suddenly.

The boy reached up with one hand, pantomiming opening the door. Dixon nodded, his weapon still in his hand.

The van rocked again, and the boy was jerked back in his seat.

"Blake," Dixon said. He flattened himself against the side of the van.

Sydney slid into position next to Dixon. The van bucked against their backs, a struggle clearly taking place inside.

"Looks like he got loose, Houdini," Sydney informed Weiss, who was still waiting down the road. "Blake and one guard are still in the van." She glanced at Dixon. He handed her a pistol and gestured toward the other side of the vehicle. She nodded and crouched low, moving around the front of the van to the passenger side.

She could hear the sounds of a struggle inside the vehicle, and it was rocking wildly with the movement of the men inside.

Sydney listened while Dixon counted down in her ear. "Three, two, one. Go!"

On his signal she stood up and shot out the passenger window, while Dixon did the same on the driver's side.

Sydney cleared the glass from the window frame. With the windows open the noise of the fight grew much louder. She glanced in quickly, taking stock of the situation.

Bazhukov was stretched over the back of the

front seat. His wrists were handcuffed together, and he had dropped them over the boy's head and was choking him.

With his arms extended, Bazhukov couldn't do much more than hang on as the boy thrashed around, trying to get away.

As the boy twisted away from the door, Dixon reached his left hand through the broken window and tripped the door locks. Bazhukov lunged toward Dixon's outstretched arm, and Dixon pulled away just in time. But in lunging, Bazhukov turned his back on Sydney, who quickly snatched the door open and put a single shot through the floorboard, less than an inch from Bazhukov's left foot.

The sound of the shot made Bazhukov freeze.

The boy, feeling the hold on his neck go slack, slid out from under Bazhukov's grip and tumbled out of the driver's side door.

"Phoenix, was that a gunshot? Outrigger, who's shooting?" Weiss asked through the comm.

"It's under control, Houdini," Sydney said, looking directly at Bazhukov.

"You missed," Bazhukov said menacingly.

"No," Sydney said. "I hit *exactly* what I wanted to. And I want the next one to go through your foot, and the one after that through your ankle. I never miss."

Bazhukov's eyes narrowed, and he looked hard at Sydney. "I've seen you before."

She gestured with the barrel of the gun and spoke to him in English. "Sit back, and let's see if we can get you out of here in one piece."

Dixon escorted the young guard to the middle of the road, had him sit down, and handcuffed him. The boy was starting to shake again, and Dixon tried to reassure him.

"You won't be hurt," he said. "We need this prisoner. Tell your superiors that Mr. Bazhukov's employers wanted to have a little chat with him."

"His employers?" the boy repeated.

"Yes. Can you remember that? Tell them we had some questions about a job he was doing for us," Dixon replied.

"But what about my partner?" the boy asked.

"Wait here," Dixon said, and went to get the other guard.

Sydney secured Bazhukov in the back of the van, bolting his shackles to the base of the bench that served as a seat, while Dixon checked on the first guard, who was starting to come to. Dixon helped him to his feet. The man was woozy and he stumbled as he crossed the road back to the van.

Sydney and Dixon took the guards' uniforms so if they were spotted they would not stand out. They escorted the two men, now wearing only long underwear, into the cargo area of the van. Bazhukov glared at all of them as Sydney and Dixon placed the guards well beyond his reach. Once all their captives were in place, Dixon climbed behind the wheel, and Sydney got in on the passenger side.

"Ready to roll, Houdini," she said.

"Roger that. I'll be waiting for you," Weiss replied.

Dixon made a three-point turn and headed back the way the van had come. Behind them the fire Sydney had set behind the overturned sedan sputtered in the grass and died, leaving a tiny circle of charred greenery. If anyone noticed the broken glass in the road, it would be blamed on the sedan. No one would know they had been there.

Dixon drove slowly, searching the tall grass at the side of the road for the narrow path that led toward the Don River. Within a hundred yards he spotted a pair of faint ruts that disappeared into a field of grass. It was barely more than a cart path.

They bounced along for another quarter mile until the path dropped down a bank, hiding them from the view of anyone on the road.

Eric Weiss waited near the bank of the river with a small helicopter painted the colors of the Russian military. It might not fool the real military, but Rostov built a lot of helicopters, and to the layperson this one wouldn't seem out of place.

Dixon stopped the van next to the water and shut off the engine. He opened the back doors and let the guards see the ignition keys in his hand. Then he threw them into the river. "There will be tourist boats on the river in another hour. Someone will find you," he told them.

Dixon glanced over at Bazhukov. "Your employer will not be pleased by your capture." He yanked Bazhukov from the van and marched him to the waiting Bell 206. Between him and Weiss they wrestled the big man into the cabin, shackled him to the seat farthest from the pilot, and strapped him into a five-point harness.

"Not standard equipment, I know," Weiss said to their prisoner as he fastened the final latch on the harness. "Since you know so much about helicopters—as you demonstrated the last time we met—I presume you know there is a luggage compartment on this bird. If you'd prefer to ride in there, I think it can be arranged."

Dixon watched as Bazhukov consider his options and came to the conclusion that none of them was good. At last he leaned back into the seat. "I think I'll stay here," he said, in English.

While Dixon and Weiss took care of Bazhukov, Sydney watched the two guards. Once they realized they really would live through the ordeal, they settled in to wait for someone to rescue them.

Weiss started the engine, warming it up and watching the instruments until they registered the proper levels.

"Ready to go, Phoenix," Weiss said through his comm.

"Roger that, Houdini," Sydney said. She turned back to the two men in the van. "Out!"

She pulled the young man out first, sitting him on the ground about fifteen yards away from the van. Then she tugged on the older man. He slid across the van floor, groaning as he registered the cold.

"You'll live," Sydney said. She pulled him to his shackled feet and walked him over to sit next to the boy. "By the time the tourist boat comes by, you should be able to get to the shore and signal them." She walked back toward the helicopter.

Dixon sat beside Bazhukov in the backseat of the helicopter. Sydney buckled into the seat next to Weiss and put on the copilot's headphones.

"Let's go," she said.

They rose a few feet off the ground, the grass around them flattening. Weiss followed the river for a few miles, then turned south, staying at a low altitude. They flew in a tense silence, watching for any sign that they had been detected. But no other aircraft appeared as they skimmed over the steppes, passing over small farming villages.

At last they could see water in the distance, and in minutes they were over the Black Sea and headed for Ordu, Turkey, at top speed. Jack was waiting for them at a safe house in Ordu, and he had some questions for Mr. Bazhukov.

Questions he fully expected to have answered.

CHAPTER 8

APO SAFE HOUSE
ORDU, TURKEY—OUTSKIRTS

Eric Weiss set the helicopter down in an empty field on the outskirts of Ordu. Sydney could see the city in the distance, built on a series of low hills. The Black Sea was calm, lapping gently at the sandy beach. For a moment Sydney wished she could lie in the sand, swim in the sea, and pretend that she lived in a world where there was no terrorism or nuclear weapons.

She hastily changed into street clothes. Her low-rise jeans and tank top would instantly label her a Western tourist—a source of American dollars, not

113

a security threat. She pulled her hair into a ponytail as she watched Dixon and Weiss unload Bazhukov from the copter.

Her thoughts strayed to the young guard she had left by the river. She wondered what Dixon had thought of him—the boy could have been only a few years older than Steven. How did Dixon continue day after day, knowing the price he was paying and what he was missing?

They got Bazhukov into another van, which they had secured for the ride into the city. Once Bazhukov was settled and securely blindfolded, Dixon hastily removed his borrowed Russian uniform and changed into his usual suit and tie.

Weiss waved from the helicopter cockpit and lifted off, leaving Sydney and Dixon to take Bazhukov to the safe house, where Jack was waiting.

Dixon drove a circuitous route as Sydney sat on the passenger side of the vehicle, turned slightly so that she could keep an eye on their prisoner.

"We did you a favor," she told Bazhukov. "You'll go to an American prison, not a Russian one." She paused, letting her words sink in. "As long as we like what you have to say, that is."

His face grew red with anger, and she soon

discovered that Russian was his native tongue. It was the language he cursed in.

"You think he'll make it to an American prison?" she asked Dixon. "Or will he end up back in Russian maximum security? I don't think the Russians take kindly to saboteurs."

Dixon glanced over at Sydney. He knew his part. "He might make it to the States. Or we could just leave him here," Dixon said. "I wonder what the Turkish authorities would think of a Russian with no papers wandering around their countryside."

Sydney kept track of Bazhukov from the corner of her vision. The implied threats were having the desired effect. Bazhukov was sweating, despite his attempts to appear impassive and despite the air-conditioning's running full blast.

She glanced out the window. It was a pretty city. The buildings were in good repair, and there was green everywhere. The hills were dotted with houses made of stucco, their red tile roofs peeking from between the lush trees. Higher hills ringed the city, and up ahead the blue waters of the Black Sea glittered.

They drove alongside a narrow canal, where a river had been channeled into a concrete path through the city. Blocks of apartment buildings rose against the blue sky, and Sydney saw a slender minaret in the distance.

Dixon turned off the main street, and the road narrowed to little more than a gravel path. They drove slowly up a hill, winding between closely packed houses. As they climbed higher, the houses grew farther apart and the view became more expansive. A misty haze hung over the distant hills, obscuring their peaks.

At last they came to a wall with a gate. Dixon stopped by the structure and spoke rapidly into a communication box sunk into the rock wall. Jack's voice answered him, faint and distorted through the tiny speaker.

The gate rolled back, and Dixon drove through. Once they were clear, the gate rolled closed behind them, locking them in.

The driveway continued up the hill, between stands of hazelnut trees, their broad green leaves shading the path.

The house looked like many of the other ones they had passed. It stood three stories tall, to take advantage of the view of the water, and was topped by a red tile roof.

Jack was waiting for them at the front door, wearing a suit and tie. His square jaw was set, and his dark eyes bored through Bazhukov as they took him out of the van and undid his blindfold.

"Welcome to Turkey, Mr. Bazhukov. Or would you prefer Blake?" Jack said. He pushed their captive roughly through the door. "We want to be hospitable, after all, since you're going to be here awhile."

Inside, he shoved Bazhukov into a room off the main hall. Through the open door Sydney glimpsed a table that was bolted to the floor, and a single hardwood chair. Steel eyelets in the floor waited for shackles to be bolted to them. Bars on the windows protected the heavy plate glass. Two impassive guards in camouflage fatigues stripped of any insignia stood just inside the door. They caught Bazhukov as he came through, and half-walked, half-carried him to the chair. His shackles were quickly fastened to the eyelets.

"Would you care for something to drink?" Jack asked, his soft voice contrasting the hard look in his eyes. Before Bazhukov could answer, Jack turned to the guards. "Get Mr. Bazhukov a soda. He must be thirsty after his long trip." He then started down the hall, motioning for Sydney and Dixon to follow him.

"You two get some rest," he said, leading them to a pair of bedrooms in the back of the house. "Weiss is returning the copter, then he's heading home. I'm going to have a little talk with our friend in the other room." He smiled, but it wasn't a pleasant expression. "Just as soon as I let him have something to drink. Perhaps a lot to drink."

Jack's face softened. "You did a good job, Sydney." He turned to his old friend. "You too, Marcus. Now I just have to make it all worthwhile."

He started to walk away, then turned back. "If you need something to eat or drink, the kitchen's on the left," he said, gesturing toward the front of the house. "And the bathroom's there." He pointed to a closed door across the hall from the bedrooms. "Not that our guest is likely to see it," he added, walking back toward the room where Bazhukov awaited him.

In the hall, he passed one of the guards coming from the kitchen with a tall plastic tumbler full of soda.

"Very good," he murmured.

He passed on into the study. He would give

Bazhukov a little time, and a lot of soda. Then they would talk.

Sydney watched her father as he walked down the hall. She heard him speak quietly to the guard carrying the soda glass, and saw him go into a room across the hall from the prisoner. She understood what her father was doing by waiting, but her every nerve cried out for immediate action. She wanted to know what Bazhukov knew, *now*. She wanted to know where the next strike would be, and what his employers were planning.

Beside her Dixon laid his hand on her arm. "Let him do his job, and let's do ours."

He nodded toward the open bedroom doors. "We may only have a couple hours. You know the rule," he said. "Sleep when you can, because you never know when you'll get another chance."

She knew he was right, and she would try to sleep, but it didn't make things any easier. Still, she was just as glad to leave the interrogation to her father. He had a ruthless streak that would get the information they needed as efficiently as possible. Dixon, Sloane, her father—each man could be as cold and hard as the job demanded. *Yet there's no arguing that every one of them, even my father, can be warm and caring with their children,* she thought.

Somehow Sloane, Jack, and Dixon managed to compartmentalize their feelings as their jobs required. Even with her, the woman who was both his colleague and his daughter, Jack seldom let his guard down. He would not allow his personal and professional lives to cross.

Sydney closed the bedroom door behind her. There was a small duffel bag on the bed, the one she had packed before she left Los Angeles. Jack had brought it to the safe house. She took out a pair of soft flannel pajamas and slowly changed. She wondered if she would ever be able to maintain the kind of emotional distance that Dixon and Jack did, without losing the ability to care for the people around her. It was such a delicate balance. But this wasn't the time or place for soul-searching. It was time to sleep and conserve her energy for whatever lay ahead.

She slept knowing that Bazhukov was in custody and because, as Dixon had said, you never knew when you would get another chance.

* * *

A knock on the bedroom door awakened Sydney. In an instant she remembered where she was and why she was there.

There must be news.

She opened the door to find her father standing in the hall, and Dixon waiting in the doorway of the second bedroom.

"What is it?" she asked.

"Mr. Bazhukov has decided that an American prison is his best alternative," Jack said. His eyes were cold, and his face gave away no hint of what had transpired while she slept.

"So, what did he say?"

"Not a lot, but enough for Marshall to work with," Jack said. He glanced at his watch. "We take off in thirty minutes. By the time we're in L.A., we should know more."

"I'll be ready in one minute," Sydney said, stepping back into the bedroom.

She swung the door shut just as Bazhukov emerged with a guard from the bathroom across the hall. She realized he was wearing a pair of pants different from the ones he had been wearing when they captured him.

He quickly averted his eyes, a flush of embarrassment passing over his features.

Clearly, Soukis hadn't told him about this part of the job.

APO HEADQUARTERS
LOS ANGELES

Marshall's work space was full. In addition to the usual clutter of computers, monitors, testing equipment, and who-knew-what, there was also a crowd of agents.

Marshall sat in the center of the crowd, his dark hair standing on end due to his continually running his fingers through it. Sydney stood behind him, watching over his shoulder as his fingers flew over his keyboard. Dixon stood to her left.

Weiss was back out in the field on another mission, but Nadia was present, standing in the corner and talking with Sloane.

Sydney's own father stood a few steps back, at the rear of the group, his face impassive. He betrayed none of the hope that the rest of them tried—unsuccessfully—not to feel.

They had been questioning Blake constantly; Vaughn was in with him now. The rest of the team was waiting for Marshall to gain access to an oil company's security files.

"You're sure that's what Blake—er, Bazhukov—said?" Marshall asked for what seemed like the hundredth time.

"Yes." The single syllable was short and crisp. Jack's impatience showed in his snappish reply.

"Okay," Marshall said. His hands never stopped moving over the keyboard. It was as though they were controlled by a separate part of his brain. "Give me a little longer . . ."

"How many more files do you have to search?" Dixon asked.

"I have three domestic production companies, but I'd like to get a couple more to confirm the data," Marshall replied.

Dixon nodded. Bazhukov had confirmed what they suspected. The platform and the refinery in Omsk were only tests. Soukis wanted to know if he could get something into an oil pipeline without it being detected. Bazhukov claimed Soukis had recruited him in Omsk, offering him a lucrative payday for "testing security" at that facility. When he had completed the work in Omsk, he was lured into a second trial on the oil platform by the promise of even more money. But he swore there had been only those two attempts, and now Marshall was checking his story against the maintenance records of domestic oil companies.

So far, Bazhukov's story checked out.

"I'm not finding anything," Marshall said, sitting back in his chair. He clenched and relaxed his fists, wiggling his fingers and flexing his wrists. "This is good for your hands," he said to no one in particular. "Helps avoid carpal tunnel. Well, it isn't really carpal tunnel that I'm worried about. It's just a repetitive stress problem that makes my hands—" He stopped talking as Vaughn entered the office.

"Do you have anything for us, Agent Vaughn?" Sloane asked.

"I do," Vaughn said evenly.

"Then perhaps you would care to share it?" Sloane prompted.

Vaughn stood perfectly still for a few seconds as all eyes turned to him. His expression told them the news was big, and it wasn't good.

"Bazhukov told me where his pickup point was for his next task, the place he was headed when the Russians arrested him." There was silence for a heartbeat. Then he continued. "Deadhorse, Alaska."

"I'm on it," Marshall said, and turned back to his computer. His fingers flew across the keys again, and within seconds, images began to appear on the screen.

"Deadhorse?" Sydney said. "I've never heard of it."

"Neither had I," Vaughn replied. "But Bazhukov insists that's the name of the city. He was told there would be a job waiting for him. His contact was supposed to meet him at the site tonight."

As the team crowded in, trying to see what was on Marshall's monitor, Arvin Sloane called for their attention.

"Perhaps we would be better served by putting this on the screen in the conference room," he said.

Marshall immediately routed the feed to the wall-size display in the conference room down the hall, and the team moved quickly to see what he had found.

The screen showed a haphazard collection of prefab buildings surrounded by dirty pickup trucks and heavy-construction and oil-field equipment. The tiny clump of buildings looked lost in a sea of blue and green as Marshall fiddled with the controls, trying to bring the picture into sharper focus.

"This," he said, "is Deadhorse, Alaska."

"There really is a Deadhorse," Dixon said. "But that doesn't tell us much."

"True," Marshall said.

He clicked rapidly through a series of screens. He stopped on another picture, this time a close-up of a weathered prefab building, its white paint flaking away to expose the boards underneath, and a plume of gray smoke curling from the metal chimney stack on the corrugated steel roof.

On the side of the building, painted lettering detailed its location: U.S. POST OFFICE, PRUDHOE BAY, AK 99734.

"Deadhorse is part of the Prudhoe Bay oil production facility—the beginning of the Alaska Pipeline," Marshall said. He paused to let that information sink in. "I think we have our target."

CHAPTER 9

Everyone was talking at once.

The map and the pictures of Deadhorse had made it clear. If Bazhukov's rendezvous was really in Deadhorse, there could be no other explanation: Soukis intended to sabotage the Trans-Alaska Pipeline.

Sloane's voice broke through the noise, once again commanding the agents' attention.

"All right. We have a working hypothesis, which is supported by the intel we have acquired. Let's act on that for now. Jack, I want you and Vaughn to go back into the interrogation room with Bazhukov and get everything you can from him." Sloane's face was grim as he looked around the room. "I don't have to tell any of you how vital that pipeline is to our national interests. If oil production is disrupted, national security is compromised, oil prices go through the roof, and the economy will take a nosedive. Chaos will ensue, and the fear that such an event will cause in the public will do untold damage."

"But what is the point?" Nadia asked. "Reducing oil production does nothing to benefit a man who makes his money shipping oil."

"Ah, but judging from Mr. Soukis's recent shopping spree, he has plans to line his pockets by bringing some marginal fields online. Those fields will be highly profitable, if he can raise oil prices sufficiently. Remember, he paid almost nothing for them."

Nadia understood. There seemed to be no limit to what some men would do in the name of greed.

"I also don't need to remind you," Sloane continued, "that Soukis is going to move in forty-eight hours. We do not have time to play games."

Sloane looked at Jack, an unspoken thought

passing between the two veteran agents. "Get the information, Jack," Sloane said evenly.

Jack gave a curt nod and left the room.

Vaughn followed on his heels, without speaking. He, too, knew his job.

"Dixon," Sloane said, continuing his assignments. "I want an operational plan for Prudhoe Bay in thirty minutes. Wheels up in ninety. Sydney, you and Nadia help Marshall. We need to know everything about what happened in the Gulf, including what the object in the pipeline was. We need to be ready."

Dixon headed for his desk, his mind already planning ahead for every scenario. Sydney watched him go, then turned to Marshall.

"What can we do?"

Thirty minutes later the team, minus Vaughn and Jack, reassembled in the conference room.

"We ran another analysis of the leak in the pipeline from the platform," Marshall said.

He stopped talking as Vaughn and Jack entered the room and took their places. Jack's face gave away nothing, but Vaughn looked troubled. In spite of her resolve to take it slow in her renewed relationship with Vaughn, Sydney felt a momentary impulse to go to his side.

She shoved the feeling aside. There might be time for them to talk later, but right now they had a job to do. In her line of work, saving lives came first, and personal relationships second. Hadn't her father, and Sloane, drilled that into her head often enough?

Marshall resumed his briefing. "As I was saying, Sydney, Nadia, and I went back over every bit of information we had regarding the platform. We cross-checked the sensor logs against what Blake told us."

"Bazhukov," Jack said under his breath.

Marshall glanced up at Jack. "Right, Bazhukov. I still think of him as Blake, since that was the guy who hijacked me, and he's kind of stuck in my brain as Blake. But you're right—"

"Mr. Flinkman," Sloane's impatient voice cut Marshall off.

Marshall gave him a sheepish look. "Sorry." He picked up the thread of his briefing again. "As I said, we went back over all the data. We are reasonably certain that Blake—Bazhukov—placed a remote-controlled robot in the pipeline. It carried a dummy charge of some kind, but I think we can expect the one in Alaska to have the real thing."

Marshall motioned to Sydney, who stood up to address the group. "The charge is likely triggered by an onboard sensor and is designed to travel a specific distance, or for a set amount of time, before it goes off. This would allow Soukis, through one of his so-called contractors, to damage a remote section of the pipeline without ever going near it. He will probably disguise the robot as one of the 'pigs' they use to regularly clean the pipe."

Nadia took over from Sydney at this point. "There are three hundred and eighty miles of pipeline that are buried, which makes that section the likely target." A diagram appeared on the screen behind her. "As you can see, the pipeline switches back and forth from aboveground to underground, depending on the terrain. We have no way of knowing where Soukis may plan to strike."

"That is why we must stop him before he can get the device into the pipeline," Dixon said. "We want to find Bazhukov's contact, put one of our people in his place, and sabotage their sabotage plans."

Sydney could see the tension in her partner's face.

"Time is short," Dixon continued, speaking rapidly. "There is a plane waiting to take us to Seattle. Prudhoe Bay is too small for one of our own planes to land without being noticed, so we will take a commercial flight out of Seattle."

Dixon handed out copies of a briefing report. "Nadia, you will accompany me to Seattle, posing as a woman with a bad past going to Deadhorse to find a job. I will be flying in as Bazhukov's replacement. He was placed on the Deadhorse crew as Blake, so from here on out he will be referred to only as Blake, to avoid any confusion. I will be posing as a coworker from the Petroleum Associates platform. The cover story is that Blake is in the hospital, recovering from a bad fall. Mr. Blake, by the way, is on his way to Mercy Hospital right now. He has agreed to spend the next few days in a full-body cast."

Dixon placed a special emphasis on the word agreed, and Sydney could imagine how Blake had been persuaded to go along with that portion of the plan. Perhaps he would need to be in that cast for more than a few days.

"Sydney and Vaughn will be on the same flight. They will be traveling as a couple of tourists, determined to have an adventurous vacation." He smiled and turned to Syd. "Remember those pictures of Deadhorse? That's where you'll be staying." He continued with the assignments. "Jack will stay here with Sloane and Marshall, working any intel we develop, and tracking Soukis's movements in the financial markets, in case there's any change.

"Sydney will be working with me on the primary objective, the pipeline robot. Vaughn, you and Nadia will be the backup team." He looked at the clock on the wall. "We should be off the ground in forty minutes. Are there any questions?"

Around the table everyone shook their heads. Most of the agents were already buried in the briefing material or making hasty notes on their own part of the plan.

As the rest of the team left the conference room, Jack hung back, until only he and Sloane were left.

"Arvin, I think I ought to be the one to go to Prudhoe," Jack said once they were alone. "Leave Dixon here to work with Marshall. I was the one who interrogated Bazhukov; I probably know him better than anyone else. I should have the best chance of passing myself off as someone who worked with him."

Sloane looked away from Jack, his eyes following Dixon, who was at his desk, holding the phone to his ear with one hand and rubbing his forehead with the other.

"You know, Jack, that sounds like a good idea. I'll talk to Dixon," Sloane said, and clapped his hand on Jack's shoulder. "You get ready to leave."

From the doorway Sydney caught the end of the conversation. She stood quietly, not willing to let on that she had heard what Sloane and her father were discussing, then she backed away a few steps.

From her vantage point just outside the door, she looked from her father to Dixon, trying to puzzle out her father's behavior. It wasn't like him to go over Dixon's head. Usually he would simply accept his assignment, and if he had a problem with it, he would challenge it head-on by speaking with Sloane *and* Dixon, together.

As she watched, Sloane approached Dixon, who was hanging up his phone. She saw Dixon make a familiar motion. He was slipping the picture of Steven and Robin back into his jacket, as he had on their flight home. She looked from Dixon to her own father. Why had Jack asked Sloane if he could replace Dixon as her partner on this mission? She didn't always trust her father's motives, especially when it came to manipulating her assignments. Did he think he needed to be there to protect her?

Jack Bristow always had a reason for his actions, and the argument he had given Sloane didn't seem to hold up. Even though Sloane had gone for it, Sydney was sure there was a lot more to it. She wanted to know what it was.

Jack was looking at Dixon from across the room as Sloane talked to his friend and fellow agent. An odd expression was on Jack's face. He looked almost as though he was worried about Dixon. Sydney remembered the picture of the kids that Dixon had hastily shoved back in his coat pocket. Was there a connection?

Sydney wanted to question her father, but there wasn't time right now. She had other things to do first.

Still, she would find out the truth. Later, when the time was right.

ALASKA AIRLINES DEPARTURE TERMINAL
SEATTLE, WASHINGTON

Sydney walked down the jetway to the waiting aircraft. Vaughn was close behind her. Her tightly fitted silver jumpsuit clung to her body, hugging every curve. Her high heels tapped against the industrial-grade carpet that covered the ramp, exaggerating her long-legged stride.

As she settled into first class, Sydney tossed her fur coat to Vaughn to stow in the overhead. Before he could do so, a flight attendant scurried over and took it from him. She ran her hands over the soft fur before hanging it carefully in a closet at the front of the first-class section.

Vaughn sat down next to Sydney, who gave him a wicked smile. "Forgot what it's like to fly commercial?" she teased in a whisper.

"It has been a while," he whispered back with a smile.

Jack boarded the plane a few minutes later with the rest of the coach passengers. He walked past his daughter without so much as a flicker of recognition. Nadia followed shortly after, equally aloof.

This flight was a regular commute for the crew

on the rigs, and they filled most of the coach seats. Only tourists flew first class. Tourists, and occasionally oil company executives. The latter usually flew their own planes, however, rather than take a commercial flight.

It was odd for Sydney to see her father in jeans, much less jeans and a plaid flannel shirt, with a heavy coat thrown over his arm. He always wore a suit, no matter what his assignment. This time, though, he had taken Dixon's place, and his oil rigger wardrobe came with the territory.

At last they were in the air, on the first leg of the trip. They would change planes in Anchorage, with about an hour layover.

Sydney and Vaughn continued the conversation they had started in the departure lounge, in front of the other passengers.

"I still don't see why you think this is the best way to spend our vacation," Sydney whined, and looked at Vaughn from under her eyelashes. "It's not like you haven't seen ice and snow before."

"And it's not like you haven't seen Las Vegas before," Vaughn countered. He didn't enjoy arguing with Sydney, even when it wasn't real. But most people would turn away from bickering strangers.

They would remember the argument, but would choose not to remember the participants. It made them anonymous in a situation where they would otherwise stand out. Prudhoe Bay didn't get a lot of tourists, and there wasn't any way to sneak in unnoticed. Their only choice was to make people want to ignore them.

By the time they landed in Anchorage, no one in the first-class cabin was willing to look at them, much less make eye contact. The coach passengers had barely even seen them on the way to their seats.

The Anchorage airport was small, but Jack managed to make himself inconspicuous. He sat in the back corner of a Starbucks on the main concourse, where he sipped a cup of plain black coffee.

Sydney, in her tight silver jumpsuit, drew admiring stares from most of the men in the terminal. Like Sydney, Vaughn, and Jack, many of them were waiting for the connecting flight to Deadhorse and Prudhoe Bay. If any of them were asked about her later, none of them would even remember that she'd had a companion. They probably wouldn't remember her face, either

According to the briefing packets that they had received, the oil crews at Prudhoe Bay rotated their schedules. Depending on the oil company and the season, they would work two or three weeks on, then have a similar stretch of time off. Most of them lived somewhere else and flew home on their weeks off. At any given time, a substantial percentage of the crews was en route to or from Prudhoe Bay. They made up the vast majority of the flight's passenger list, and they were overwhelmingly male.

When their flight was called, Sydney and Vaughn once again boarded with the first-class passengers. They took their seats quietly and spoke very little during the short flight to Deadhorse. If they hadn't sufficiently established their cover as tourists, there was little they could do about it now.

They had little to worry about. No one paid any attention to them. Many of the passengers were too absorbed in their own concerns to notice the tourists. It was like the subway train that led to APO Headquarters in Los Angels—a public transport full of commuters. They ogled the hot woman in the tight jumpsuit and risked a dirty look from her boyfriend, but beyond that, they didn't much care.

CHAPTER 10

ARCTIC CIRCLE HOTEL AND CAFÉ
DEADHORSE, ALASKA

Sydney eyed the one double bed in the room she shared with Vaughn. When they had made their reservation, in the names of Jerry Butler and Marci Franklin, a double was all that was available. Even though they would sleep at different times, it still made her feel uncomfortable.

She and Vaughn had gotten back together after the death of Lauren, Vaughn's double-crossing wife, but Sydney was still determined that they take their time rebuilding their relationship. There was too much history between them, too many lies and betrayals. She was still not ready to trust her feelings for Vaughn. Or his for her.

Sydney picked up her cell phone and dialed a number. Her sister answered.

"Hello? Is this Marie?" Sydney asked.

"Marie's not here. Can I take a message?"

"No, no. Nothing important. I'll call her later."

She hung up. As far as anyone tracing the call knew, she had called a residence in the south end of Seattle.

She turned to Vaughn. "Nadia is in place. My father will be in touch as soon as he meets his contact. Until then, we just have to play tourists."

Not that there was much to see. The city of Deadhorse was little more than a cluster of prefab buildings, set on the flat tundra of the Arctic Circle.

Lake Colleen, a flat, featureless expanse of freezing water, stretched between the city of Deadhorse and the oil rigs. Sydney had seen the rigs from the Deadhorse "taxi," a battered fifteen-passenger van that had met them at the airport. They hadn't called the taxi. It had just appeared, sitting in the snow outside the terminal, its wheezing engine blowing clouds of steam into the icy air.

The ride to the hotel had taken only a few minutes, during which the driver had called their attention to all the sights Deadhorse had to offer—the general store that also housed the post office, and the oil company housing where he dropped off the other passengers (including Jack). He had also pointed out a sign that proudly proclaimed FUTURE SITE OF AM/PM MINI MART. Below the sign, on the pole that held the Mini Mart announcement, were mileage markers. Deadhorse was more than three thousand miles from nearly every major city: London, Tokyo, Moscow, New York, Dallas. Even Los Angeles was, according to the sign, 2,777 miles away. It was exactly in the middle of nowhere.

To Sydney, the whole place looked like a giant run-down truck stop at the edge of the known world.

Vaughn glanced at his watch. "We have about three hours of daylight left. I think Mr. Butler would be anxious to see what he's paid all this money for." He offered her his arm, and reached for the door. "Care to take in the sights of beautiful downtown Deadhorse?"

"I think," she answered, "Ms. Franklin would

be bored silly with this place. But she might be persuaded to explore just a bit, with the promise of a nice hot toddy afterward. After all"—she stopped, grabbing a pair of heavy boots–"there's two feet of snow on the ground."

Vaughn smiled. "Ah, but remember, Ms. Franklin, that this is a dry town. You'll have to settle for hot chocolate, or a nice cup of tea. I don't know if we could even find a latte up here."

Sydney pulled a heavy fur-lined parka over her jumpsuit and slid her feet into her boots. The hotel was warm, but outside, the temperature was five or six degrees below zero, and the wind was picking up. She made sure her earpiece was secure. Jack would be online soon, and she had to be ready whenever she was needed.

In the meantime she and Vaughn would explore whatever the city of Deadhorse had to offer.

TRANS-ALASKA PIPELINE TERMINAL PRUDHOE BAY, ALASKA

Jack carried his duffel into the sparsely furnished room that served as crew quarters in Prudhoe Bay. The sharp sting of disinfectant cleaner assaulted his nose and brought tears to his eyes. But it didn't completely mask the musty odor that permeated the room, which smelled as though it never got a breath of fresh air.

The single bed was topped by a thin, bare mattress, and what he hoped was a set of clean sheets had been left on the foot of the bed. It appeared that housekeeping services were minimal.

Many of the crew rooms were doubles, but Blake had been assigned a single. That reinforced what they already knew: Blake was getting special treatment.

Jack quickly stowed the clothes and gear he had packed. His real gear would be completely out of place in his crew quarters. It was with Sydney, except for the tiny transmitter plugged into his ear. He would retrieve the rest of his tools when he needed them. In the meantime he would look and act the part of Blake's stand-in.

Following the instructions Blake had given him, Jack made his way to the common room, where he was to wait for his contact. As instructed, he sat at the table in front of the orange-juice dispenser, with a cup of black coffee.

Jack looked around. Although he appeared casual, his sharp glance took in the details of the room, noted the location of the exits, and catalogued everyone who came and went. If he had to, he would be able to remember every man and woman he saw.

The room itself was a single large unit, linked by enclosed corridors to the rest of the housing complex. The walls were a plastic-coated composite common to temporary buildings, a featureless expanse of textured white. The floor was linoleum, or a close relative. There were large worn spots under each chair, mute testimony to the constant traffic. With long work days and multiple shifts, someone was always coming or going.

A man approached Jack's table and pulled out the chair opposite him. He was tall and lean, and he sported a luxuriant handlebar mustache. Jack had already noticed that most of the men on the rig were not clean-shaven. He wondered if the facial hair helped keep them warm in the subzero temperatures.

They sat in silence for a few long minutes, the stranger looking hard at Jack. The man·emptied his coffee cup and drew out a pack of cigarettes and a lighter. With a casual nod he offered the pack to Jack.

Jack shook his head. "Trying to quit," he said, giving Blake's signal.

"You don't look like him," the stranger said.

"I'm not." Jack leaned forward, keeping his voice low. "Our mutual friend had a bad fall. He's in the hospital in Los Angeles and can't do the job. He told me about it, said he'd set it up for me to take over."

The man leaned back and took a drag on his cigarette, watching Jack through the stream of smoke as he exhaled. "Well, he didn't. Set it up, I mean. Don't know nothin' about a substitute."

Jack shrugged. "Said he'd do it. Doesn't mean he did. But he is in the hospital in L.A. And he did tell me there was a big payday at the end of the job. Didn't tell me much else, except that he was sure I could handle it."

"How could he know that?"

"We worked together on the offshore platform. Got to know each other pretty good," Jack replied. He crossed his arms over his chest and leaned back, keeping his posture deliberately casual.

"So you don't know what's involved here?" the man asked.

"Nope. Just said there was a big payday. Figured I didn't need to know much more than that," Jack said.

"So, Blake'll vouch for you?"

"I expect he will. But why don't you just check with him? He's in Mercy Hospital," Jack said.

"Just might do that," the man said, rising from his chair. "Wait here."

It didn't sound like a suggestion.

"I guess I'll wait here," Jack said under his breath as the man walked away. He had never even told Jack his name, but Jack would have it soon enough.

Jack quietly repeated a concise description of the man, which went out over the comm to the entire Deadhorse team: Sydney, Vaughn, and Nadia.

Sydney flipped open her cell phone. After her call to Nadia, Marshall had been able to establish an encrypted cell phone line. Without a reliable, secure satellite link to headquarters, it was their only open line of communication from the remote Arctic wilderness. Sydney quickly relayed the description, and the results of the conversation to Dixon.

In Los Angeles, Dixon and Marshall immediately started a search of the oil company personnel records. As Marshall brought up names that matched the description, Dixon checked them against the current roster.

Meanwhile, Jack waited. It was part of the job, and he could wait for hours if he had to, even though his brain kept ticking off the minutes, warning him of the deadline. He stayed calm by reminding himself that the plan couldn't go through without him. Nothing could happen until headquarters and the rest of his team decided what to do. That would be the time for action, and not before.

Sydney's phone rang. Dixon's voice came over the line. "Mr. Blake has a visitor."

MERCY HOSPITAL
LOS ANGELES, CALIFORNIA

The APO team in Los Angeles was monitoring Blake's hospital room with a camera. There was a transmitter hidden in the headboard of his hospital bed, and Eric Weiss, disguised as a maintenance man, was repairing an outlet in the room across the hall. From there he had a clear view of Blake.

At APO headquarters Dixon watched the feed from the camera as the visitor approached the bed. Blake was encased in plaster, his head swathed in bandages that obscured his whole face except for his mouth, his nostrils, and one eye. His legs were slightly elevated, raised in slings and held in place by a series of pulleys. Clearly, he wasn't going anywhere.

Dixon chose not to wonder whether any of the bandages were actually necessary. It didn't matter to him. He listened to the visitor greet Blake in Greek, then switch to English.

"The boss wanted me to stop in and see how you were. He said you had a bad fall," the man said. He paused and looked Blake up and down. "But he didn't say how bad."

Blake tried to gesture with one plaster-covered arm, then groaned with the effort. He inhaled deeply, as though steadying himself. When he spoke, it was little more than a breathy whisper escaping from between his chapped lips. "Yeah. Not going anywhere for a while."

"I heard you got a guy to cover your job in Prudhoe for you. Man, those spots pay good. Musta really busted your chops to give up that change," the visitor said.

Blake nodded, a tiny movement of the swath of bandages. "Water," he croaked.

The man looked around and spotted a glass with a straw on the bedside table. He held it out to Blake, then realized the patient couldn't hold it to his mouth. The visitor held it up, and Blake took a sip.

"Better," Blake said. His voice sounded a little stronger. "Yeah, I got a guy from Louisiana to cover for me. I hate to give up the bucks, but he promised me a cut, so I sent some work his way."

The visitor put the glass back on the table and settled into a chair next to the bed. He seemed to be making himself at home, as if he expected to stick around for a while. "So, what do you know about this guy?" he asked.

Blake might have shrugged, but the plaster didn't move. "His name's Matt. Knows his way around a rig. Knows how to keep his mouth shut. I figured that was enough." He stopped and drew a shallow breath. "You didn't know no more'n that about me."

"You might be surprised how much we know," the man replied.

There was a shadow of menace in the simple declaration.

Watching from headquarters, Dixon considered

creating an interruption, but he waited for Blake's response.

"Hell, there ain't much more to know about me. But, if you say so . . ." His voice trailed off.

"Yeah. Well." The man reached into his jacket pocket.

Dixon tensed. Weiss's comm crackled for an instant, then the agent spoke. "I'm on it."

On the video screen in front of Dixon, a solidly built man in a maintenance uniform stepped into the view of the camera.

"Did you call about a dripping faucet?" Weiss asked.

The visitor turned, his hand still partially sticking out of his pocket. He turned back to Blake, his hand continuing to emerge from his jacket.

Weiss approached the bed, rushing the visitor. He grabbed the man's arm and twisted it behind his back.

The man yelped in pain. He dropped the cell phone he had pulled from his pocket.

"What in the hell are you doing?"

"Oh, man. I'm sorry. We don't allow cell phones in patient rooms. It's a safety issue, man, like the place will blow up or something. I just reacted."

Weiss grabbed the phone off the floor, and wiped imaginary dust from the keys. "I am so sorry, really. I mean, I just—" He sputtered, looking horrified. "You don't have to tell my boss, do you? I mean, I'm new here. Just started last week, and I'm tryin' to follow all the rules." A note of bitterness crept into his voice. "He'll fire my ass for sure." Weiss handed the phone back to the visitor.

Blake's guest held up a palm toward the agent. "No harm, no foul. I'll take it to the lobby. Relax, man."

Weiss backed out of the room, his hands raised innocently in front of him. "Thanks, man. I owe ya."

He retreated into the hall, then turned and walked to the end of the corridor and ducked around a corner, where he couldn't be seen from Blake's room.

"There's a tracker on the cell," he said, watching around the corner for the visitor.

"Good," Dixon said. "Fast thinking to tag the phone, once we knew what it was."

"Thanks," Weiss replied.

"We'll track his call. Marshall has the hospital security monitors on here. Once he's clear of the building, I want you back here immediately," Dixon said. "We'll leave a security guard on Blake, just in case his visitor returns."

"Roger that," Weiss answered. He chuckled softly. "Maybe I should go finish that outlet while I'm waiting."

Dixon smiled and went back to searching for the identity of Jack's new friend on the rig.

APO HEADQUARTERS LOS ANGELES

Marshall gave Dixon two more names to check. The second one was a hit—all the details were right. The man was in Prudhoe Bay this week, but he wasn't supposed to be on duty at this hour. He fit the description, and his work history included a stint with a Soukis subsidiary in the Middle East.

Dixon dialed Sydney's cell phone and quickly brought her up to speed. Now that the line was secure, it was the most efficient way to communicate between headquarters and the field.

"Our man's name is Rodney Chambers. He was born in Oklahoma and raised all over the world. His father worked rigs wherever he could find a job, with Rodney and his mother tagging along. Dad worked on the pipeline construction crew when Rodney was a kid, so Rodney knows the project and the area." Dixon paused as Marshall uploaded additional intel on their subject. "He has anger issues that have cost him a few jobs, and he has a reputation as a troublemaker. But he's kept his nose clean in Prudhoe, so far. There's nothing in his file to indicate he might be involved in anything questionable."

Sydney listened carefully and repeated back each bit of information for the benefit of Vaughn, who stood beside her listening, her father, who was still waiting in the common room of the crew quarters, and Nadia, who was posted nearby.

"If it is him," Dixon said, "he has a tattoo of a crescent moon on his left wrist. Ask Jack if he can confirm that."

Sydney repeated the question. On the other end of the comm link, Jack Bristow grunted. "Yes," he said softly. Then his voice coarsened and he said more loudly, "You're back."

Sydney spoke into her cell phone. "He says it's him, and he's back. I'll report in as soon as there's more information."

"Right. Take care of yourself." Dixon hung up, breaking the connection.

TRANS-ALASKA PIPELINE TERMINAL
PRUDHOE BAY, ALASKA

Jack sat back as the man he now knew was Rodney Chambers approached the table. The success of the mission depended on Chambers's accepting him as a substitute for Blake. He didn't want to appear too eager. He should be a little impatient, a little bored and annoyed at waiting. It was all in the attitude.

Jack looked at his watch, then back up at Chambers. He let the gesture speak for itself, saying nothing as Chambers sat back in the chair across the table. Chambers stared at him. Jack waited, keeping his expression flat and neutral.

At the other end of the comm, Sydney waited, hearing only silence. She looked at Vaughn, who shook his head. He didn't like the silence either, but all they could do was wait.

If Jack needed backup, he would let them know. Until then, they were to maintain their position, strolling through the streets of Deadhorse.

Jack cleared his throat. The noise was loud in Sydney's ear after the long minutes of silence. He still didn't speak.

"Raptor, this is Phoenix. We're still here," Sydney said, even though she knew her father wouldn't reply.

Jack didn't fidget. He didn't look around the room, he didn't get up and refill his coffee; he just waited. He'd had a lot of practice. He knew he could wait out anyone. Chambers was no exception.

Finally Jack spoke. "Our friend got busted up pretty good, according to my sources." He leaned forward, resting his elbows on the chipped plastic tabletop. "He fell off a pump, or so I heard. Don't know how he got that careless—he's not a careless kind of guy—but he didn't tell me that. He just said for me to come up here and there would be a job waiting."

"There is," Chambers said. He stuck his hand out to Jack. "The guys call me Rod, by the way. Now tell me what you know about the layout up here, and then I'll give you the nickel tour."

"Sure. Mind if I get some more coffee first?" Jack asked.

"Go ahead," Chambers replied. He smiled, or at least that's what Jack thought he was trying to do. It wasn't a cheery sight. "Bring me a cup too, would you? Black, double sugar."

"Sure," Jack said. He pushed his chair back and walked across the worn linoleum to the coffee station. He took his time pouring two cups and adding sugar.

"It's a go. Shotgun, get your backup in position." Jack spoke softly, his back to where Chambers sat at the table.

"Got it, Raptor," Vaughn answered. "Phoenix will call Outrigger and Merlin. I'll be in touch."

Jack walked back to the table with the two cups of coffee and put one down in front of Chambers. He sat back down and took a sip, careful not to make a face at the taste. How long, he wondered, had that stuff been sitting there?

"Well, Rod," Jack began. Using the man's first name did not come naturally to the normally reserved agent, but he forced himself to relax and play the part. "Let me tell you what I know."

Jack began to recite facts and figures about the pipeline and its construction history: when it was built, the special challenges of working in the extreme environment—stuff any pipeline worker should know. Jack had done his homework, and it paid off. He proved he was on the inside of Soukis's operation.

TRANS-ALASKA PIPELINE TERMINAL
PRUDHOE BAY, ALASKA

Jack followed Rod Chambers into the crew shed at the pumping station. Rod handed him a set of high-visibility coveralls from the uniform rack, and Jack pulled them on over his rough work clothes. He tried not to think about who might have worn them before him or how long it had been since they were cleaned.

As he zipped up the coveralls, his back was to Rod. He slipped a tiny transmitter from his pocket and stuck it to the top of the uniform rack. Everything that was said in the room would be broadcast to the team.

Because of the extreme weather, the North Slope rigs were all enclosed in large boxlike structures. They were utilitarian at best, with few amenities.

From the outside, the buildings gave little clue to their function. They were a flat beige color that blended in with the scrubby vegetation of the tundra. The distinctive pumps and well rigging were all enclosed, hidden from the casual observer and protected from the elements.

Without that protection, both the rigs and the workers would quickly freeze in the subzero temperatures on the shore of the Arctic Ocean. It was a harsh environment, one that challenged even the hardiest individuals—an isolated, dangerous strip of civilization chiseled from the unforgiving landscape.

But once you were inside, the rigs were like every other drilling rig. The same field of wellheads, the same maze of pipes and pumps, the same underlying hum of activity that marked any drill site. Except that this site controlled the flow of oil from one of the richest fields in the country—a flow that was vital to the financial and industrial health of the nation.

And someone—someone greedy and unscrupulous—was trying to interrupt that flow.

Jack followed Rod through his routine as his new acquaintance checked the wellheads and pumps for signs of leaks or damage and reviewed the safety logs from the previous shift.

The irony was not lost on Jack: One of the rig's safety officers was Soukis's man on the inside. From Soukis's point of view, it made perfect sense.

As they made their way through the buildings, Rod kept up a steady stream of one-sided conversation. He didn't seem to pay any attention when Jack occasionally hung back, running his hand over a piece of machinery or reading a safety poster. It didn't appear to bother him that Jack seldom spoke, or that when Jack did speak, he merely repeated bits of information that Marshall had given him via Sydney and her cell phone.

And Sydney, along with the rest of the team, was listening to every word Jack said, and relaying it back to Dixon and Marshall.

"This is the beginning of the pipeline," Rod said as he passed a series of pumps and tanks. "It's where we put the pigs in the line to clean it," he went on, referring to the dumbbell-shaped devices that regularly scoured the inside of the pipeline.

The pig access itself was a gap in the pipe. The incoming pipe curved into a bypass, and a stub pipe entered the line at the far end of the curve. The end of the stub had a removable access hatch, where the pig would be loaded into the pipe and then released into the line. At the takeout points along the line there would be two stubs, one to allow a pig to be removed, and one to allow an insertion, like the stub in Prudhoe Bay.

Chambers gestured to a control station with monitoring screens and gauges that overlooked the pig bypass. "And this is the station where we monitor their progress and track any obstructions in the line. This ain't your normal assignment, but it's where you'll work tonight."

They continued on for a bit, then doubled back to the monitoring station.

Rod stopped to look over the station. "Of course, you won't see anything on the monitors. But you'll still have to watch 'em when you're on duty."

Jack slowly scanned the area. It was a sparse L-shaped tabletop, lined with a half-dozen video and computer monitors. The video monitors showed grainy black-and-white images of workers in coveralls like his, which looked dusty gray on the monochrome screens.

One of the monitors was focused on the pig access point they had just passed. Another displayed the lines of wellheads as workers made their way between them, visually inspecting them for signs of damage or leaks. In an operation as sensitive as this, nothing was left to chance, and double- and triple-checking everything was a matter of course.

The computer displays monitored pressure and temperature readings from stations along the pipeline. The readings supplemented the regular visual inspection of the eight-hundred-mile-long line and were used to identify potential trouble spots.

At least that was what they were *supposed* to do.

Something in Chambers's voice made Jack stop. Clearly, there *would* be something to see. Just as clearly, his job was to not see it.

Jack nodded toward the pumps. "Just a long shift of watching nothing, eh?"

Rod winked. "Not a thing, buddy. Not a thing."

Rod walked away from the monitoring station, his back to Jack.

Jack casually slid his hand through the side slit in his coveralls and into his pants pocket. He found the tiny device he was looking for and swiftly reached out, his hand deftly slipping behind the monitoring station. Within seconds the bug's bonding compound was released and it was firmly attached to a hidden spot on the station. If anything happened before Jack came back, the team would know about it.

Jack continued to follow Rod through the facility, leaving occasional bugs in his wake. He felt fairly certain the monitoring station was the target, since he would be assigned there and since Chambers had been so emphatic that there would be nothing for him to see, also implying that should anyone else walk by his job would be to make sure they didn't see anything either. Still, there was a chance that Soukis, or whoever had given the go-ahead for Jack to replace Blake, hadn't completely bought his story and that Jack was being distracted while the actual sabotage took place somewhere else.

The more APO heard, the better they could respond.

ARCTIC CIRCLE HOTEL AND CAFÉ
DEADHORSE, ALASKA

Sydney adjusted her cell phone headset and addressed Dixon across the secure channel. "Outrigger, this is Phoenix. How do you read?" She was going to meet Jack an hour before his shift at the monitoring station to do surveillance. Jack planned on getting to "work" a bit early, but in the meantime he and the rest of the team wanted to make sure they weren't missing anything.

"Loud and clear, Phoenix."

"All right. I'm leaving now. Raptor is waiting for me."

She pulled her coat tight around her and stepped out into the hallway. Vaughn had left an hour earlier to meet Nadia. The two of them would be Sydney and Jack's backup team.

It was a little after seven, and the night sky was dark. She knew it would be light for another hour or more back in Los Angeles, but above the arctic circle, nightfall was early. And cold.

Sydney was dressed in layers of high-tech clothing designed for the subzero temperatures. Although the mercury hovered around zero most of the day, at night it would drop to as low as minus ten, and the wind chill could send it even lower. She carried an additional layer of clothing in case the temperature became too unbearable, the super-lightweight fabric stuffed in a pack strapped around her waist. The fur-lined parka she had worn earlier was slung over her arm. She slipped it on and fastened it before opening the outer door.

Deadhorse at night was an eerie sight. There was a deep blanket of snow on the ground, with ruts marking where the roads passed through the area. Across the lake she could see the lights on the rigs, and the sounds of the crews working carried faintly from the distance.

Freezing air stung her nostrils as she inhaled, and the cold moved down into her lungs with each breath. She pulled her hood closed over the lower half of her face, trying to warm the air she breathed. With each exhalation, trails of steam wafted from her nose.

The night was clear, with plumes of smoke and steam glowing in the light from the rigs. Sydney made her way between the shrouded buildings, avoiding the lights of the twenty-four-hour hardware store that served as the social center of Deadhorse.

She reached the prearranged rendezvous point,

where Jack waited in a battered pickup truck with the engine running.

In the cab of the truck the heater ran full blast, fighting with only marginal success to keep the cold from seeping in. As Sydney opened the door, a wave of warm air washed over her, and she scrambled into the relative shelter of the cab.

Without a word Jack pulled away from the ramshackle collection of buildings and drove the short distance around the lake. Anywhere else they would have walked, but at these temperatures no one exposed themselves to the frigid air unless they absolutely had to.

Jack parked the truck alongside a row of similar vehicles in a graveled parking area near the crew shack. The shift change had taken place an hour earlier, while he was touring the facility with Rod. Now the parking lot was quiet and dark, and the crew was safely inside the rig, out of the bitter cold. Jack and Sydney climbed from the truck in silence and made their way to a small warehouse building at the edge of the parking area. During the summer it served as a storage facility for road maintenance supplies. Now, with the onset of winter, it had been abandoned until spring. It was a perfect observation post.

Nadia and Vaughn were in a similar building a half mile away. They had receivers tuned to the bugs Jack had planted earlier. Back in Los Angeles, Marshall had hacked his way into the security system in order to give them a visual feed, but the images were of poor quality and had no audio.

It was only the combination of Jack's short-range bugs, the poor-quality video surveillance, and the agents on the ground that gave the team a true picture of what was going on inside the blank walls of the rig.

Jack and Sydney settled themselves on a pair of packing crates. Vaughn had left them a small oil heater when he scouted the place, and they sat with it between them.

"Do you think anything will happen tonight?" Sydney asked, stretching her gloved hands toward the heater.

Jack was watching the parking area through a small window. "From the way Chambers acted, yes." He kept staring into the darkness, alert for any unusual movement.

"He didn't buy your story, did he?"

Jack shook his head. "I can't be sure. He showed me the facility, told me what I was going to do, and acted as though I was on the inside of the operation, but I don't think he told me everything."

"But that could just be prudence," Sydney said. She stood up and moved her crate closer to where her father was sitting. "Don't tell the little guy any more than he has to know."

"True," Jack said. "Still, there's always the chance they didn't believe my story and they'll change their plans. Whatever they do, we need to be ready."

A movement near their truck caught Sydney's eye. She grabbed her night-vision goggles and peered into the darkness.

Someone was prowling around the truck.

Jack had seen the movement too, and he edged away from the window, moving slowly toward the door.

"Can you identify them?" he asked. He spoke softly, his words much louder in Sydney's headset than in the room.

"Negative," she whispered, training her goggles on the front of the truck. Whoever it was, he seemed to be most interested in the engine, which was still warm from their short drive.

"Wait!" Sydney hissed as the image became clear.

Jack froze, his hand on the doorknob.

Sydney giggled. She couldn't help it.

"Phoenix? This is Evergreen. What's going on?" Nadia's voice came over the comm from her post.

"This is Outrigger. What's the problem?" Dixon's worried voice came through on the cell phone headset as well.

Jack stared at her expectantly from his spot near the door.

"This is Phoenix," she said, the giggles subsiding. "No problem. There isn't anyone out there."

Jack shook his head in confusion. He had seen the movement, just as she had.

"It's a bear," Sydney said. "And not a very big one." She paused to let the information sink in to her audience. "He's moving off now. He must not have wanted anything in the truck."

Jack moved back from the door and returned to his post on the packing crate. For a few minutes neither father nor daughter spoke.

Sydney carefully muted her transmitter and covered the mouthpiece of the cell phone. "Dad?"

Jack looked at his daughter. Something in her tone and in her face told him this was not a conversation to be shared with the rest of the team. He muted his transmitter also—he could key it open in a fraction of a second if necessary.

"What are you doing here?" There was a note of challenge in Sydney's question, as though she expected an argument, not an answer.

"Waiting for Chambers to make his move," Jack answered, not giving anything away. "Just like you."

"That isn't what I meant, and I think you know that," Sydney said. She hesitated, then plunged ahead. "And I don't think that's what you're doing. Or at least it isn't all you're doing. You weren't supposed to be here. Sloane assigned Dixon to this mission."

Jack didn't look at her. "It's an assignment. I was the best man for the job. Sloane understood that when I pointed it out, and he made the call. Nothing more."

"But there is more," Sydney continued. Her voice had a note of pleading in it. "Dixon would have been fine on this mission. He's my partner. Why did you have him pulled off so you could take his place?"

"I thought I was best for the job, Sydney," Jack said again, then closed his mouth in a firm line.

Sydney shook her head. She could be as

stubborn as her father. After all, where did he think she had learned it?

"I don't buy that. You want to know what I think? I think it has something to do with me," Sydney said. She stared at him in the dim light. "Did you do it to put yourself between me and Vaughn? Because it won't work."

Jack sighed. "Let it go, Sydney."

"I learned my interrogation techniques from the best, Dad," Sydney said. "And you haven't given me all the answers. Yet."

Jack couldn't suppress a faint, sad smile. "You're right, Sydney, and you're very, very wrong. I truly believe I am the best person for this mission, and I would not have asked to replace Dixon otherwise. There is no way I would jeopardize any mission, no matter now trivial or how important, for personal reasons."

Sydney knew that was true. She had seen her father sacrifice his own health, his wife, even his daughter, when a mission required it. There was nothing that would come between Jack and his devotion to his duty.

"I will admit," Jack continued, "that there was another reason, and it does have to do with your relationship. But not in the way you think."

Jack drew a deep breath as Sydney sat completely still. She remained silent, letting her father get to his explanation in his own time. Any interruption and he would clam up, as he always did.

"Dixon is a good man, Sydney. One of the best men I have ever known. I would trust him with my life, and yours. And I have on many occasions. But I didn't want him on this mission," Jack said.

"But why? So you could interfere with me and Vaughn?" Sydney asked.

"It has nothing to do with Vaughn. It's about Dixon," Jack said softly. "Dixon and his family. Dixon and Steven and Robin."

Jack stood up, waving for Sydney to take his place at the window. Unable to sit still for this conversation, he paced the floor behind her, talking quietly.

"They're good kids, but they've been through a lot, and Steven's in trouble at school."

Sydney fought the impulse to turn around. "How do you know that?" she asked without moving.

"I overheard him talking to Marshall. One father to another, talking about their kids." Regret tinged Jack's words as he continued. "It was the kind of conversation he should have had with me, but I don't think I was the kind of father he wants to emulate."

"You could have done worse," Sydney said. "You did the best you knew how."

She wasn't sure she believed her own words, after all the things her father had done, but this wasn't the time nor place to have that conversation. Besides, she *wanted* to believe it was true, and that was enough for now.

"I'm not sure I did, but that's not really the point," Jack said. His tone turned brisk. "The point is, Steven needs a strong parent right now. This job, Dixon's job, has already cost those children their mother. So, right now Steven needs his father. He needs Dixon more than we do. And Dixon needs him."

"What do you mean?" Sydney asked.

"Those kids are Dixon's anchor, his foundation. They are what held him together when Diane was killed. Not the job, not finding her killer, not his colleagues or his friends. Knowing the kids needed him kept him going when nothing else would. They keep him grounded," Jack said.

Sydney kept her eyes on the landscape outside the tiny window, but her thoughts went back to her own childhood with Jack and Irina. Her parents had

had jobs like Dixon's, with the same dangers and the same costs. How had they managed? How had they made time to be parents, with the demands of their jobs? How did anyone, for that matter?

But they had made time, and her father had cared for her when her mother went away. Had *she* been the thing that kept Jack grounded? Was *she* the reason he'd made it through the dark days after Irina's betrayal was revealed?

"Dad?" Sydney's voice was small in the darkened warehouse. "Dad, was it like that for you? Is that why you feel this way about Dixon? Because someone kept you grounded?"

She knew it was risky to ask her father such a direct question, especially one so fraught with emotional significance. Jack buried his feelings deep inside himself and didn't let anyone see them—least of all his daughter. She didn't really expect an answer. And she didn't get one.

Jack continued to pace, but he said nothing. Sydney was used to it. Life as Jack Bristow's daughter had always meant long stretches of silence. This was just one more.

After pacing for a few minutes, Jack came back over to the window and nudged her aside. "My turn," he said, taking over the vigil at the window.

Sydney put her transmitter back on broadcast mode and uncovered the cell phone. She would try to talk to her father again later. She could be as persistent as he was. But she knew she had gotten all she could from him for now.

"This is Phoenix," she said, her voice going out to the rest of the team, including the crew at headquarters. "Anything happening out there?"

"This is Shotgun. All quiet here," Vaughn answered from his post.

"Outrigger here. Aside from Marshall trying to redesign the oil rig's video surveillance system by remote control, nothing here," Dixon said.

Sydney had to smile. She could imagine Marshall's impatience with the poor quality of the images they were receiving, and she knew he would be tweaking every setting he could in an attempt to improve the feed. He couldn't help himself.

"Roger that, Outrigger. Let me know if he succeeds," Sydney said.

"Will do," Dixon replied. His voice was somber as he continued. "So far all we have is normal activity. The crew has meal breaks staggered throughout the next ninety minutes. That may be the critical time, while there are more people moving around and fewer people actually working."

"Roger that, Outrigger," Sydney said, then relayed the message to the rest of the team through her comm.

The line went quiet. Sydney's eyes had adjusted to the dark interior of the storage shed, and she could see the silhouettes of crates stacked against the walls. Everything was packed away for the winter. If it hadn't been for the new carefully printed labels on each crate, she would have thought the place was abandoned.

She concentrated on the constant feed of industrial noises coming from inside the rig. She could hear the steady hum of pumps and heaters and the chime of regulators as they clocked the volume of the oil flow. It was the sound of a well-run facility, sending vital oil out along eight hundred miles of pipeline to the port of Valdez, where it would be loaded onto tankers.

A bell clanged, signaling the first meal break. Within minutes she could hear a hum of conversation in the crew shed as the men filed in.

She had not seen the chow line, but Jack had described it to her: a cafeteria-style serving line open around the clock, with standard buffet fare. He had noted that the dessert case was opened every few seconds, but the fruit case looked untouched. It was that kind of crowd.

Jack tapped Sydney on the shoulder and gently led her to the window. The sky was full of twisting bands of color.

The Northern Lights.

She had heard of them, but she had never seen them, and the sight was overwhelming. A spiral of green light twisted in the sky like a ghostly tornado, bathing the ground in a pale green glow. It moved with a sinuous grace, turning lazy pirouettes before it faded and disappeared.

Sydney cleared her throat and muted her transmitter again. She intended to take this opportunity to try once more to talk with her father. She still wanted answers. But just as she was about to open her mouth, the bell clanged inside the rig, signaling the beginning of another meal shift. The production floor maintained its hum, and the chatter in the break room continued.

But there was another noise. One they had not heard before.

The sound of hushed voices.

They heard someone ask, "Are your people in place?"

"This is Raptor," Jack said into his comm. "That's Chambers. Something's happening."

"Roger that, Raptor," Vaughn answered.

"Merlin, this is Phoenix," Sydney said. "Do you have anything on visual?"

"Phoenix, this is Merlin. I have some really rotten video, but it looks like there are two guys carrying a satchel onto the floor. Looks like a pig—well, not a real pig. You know, one of those cleaning pigs they use in the pipe—"

"Merlin, do you have access to the maintenance schedules? Is there anything scheduled for tonight?" Sydney asked.

"Negative, Phoenix. I mean, affirmative on the access, negative on the schedule. Nothing for another week," Marshall replied.

"This is Outrigger," Dixon broke in. His voice carried authority. "This is not a scheduled operation. I want everyone in there. Now!"

"Roger," Sydney replied. She was already at the door, ready to move as she quickly relayed instructions to the backup team.

"Shotgun and Evergreen in position," Vaughn

said. "Ready to move on your signal, Phoenix."

"Roger that," Sydney said, and nodded to Jack.

"Go!" Dixon said.

Sydney ran out the door, with Jack at her heels. She alerted Vaughn and Nadia as she raced across the hundred yards to the entrance to the facility. There was no one around to see them, and at the moment speed was more important than stealth. They streaked between the collection of trucks in the parking lot, toward the south side of the complex.

From the other direction Vaughn and Nadia were mirroring their movements.

"Raptor, this is Shotgun. We are at the north entrance."

"Roger that, Shotgun. We are at the south. Go on my mark. We'll take the monitoring station, you take the pumps."

"Copy that, Raptor."

Jack and Sydney had reached the door to the facility. Jack nodded at Sydney and spoke to Vaughn and Nadia on the comm.

"Mark," he said.

Sydney opened the door and stepped inside. Jack followed her.

Behind her Jack talked softly into his comm.

"Remember, no gunfire inside. It's too dangerous."

The room with the uniforms was deserted. They crossed the well field, the now-familiar wellheads looking strangely out of place indoors, then passed through the central power station at a brisk and purposeful walk. Although she wanted to run, Sydney forced herself to keep the deliberate pace—there was no need to draw attention to themselves.

Two minutes later they arrived at the monitoring station, after walking through a series of compartments. As she walked, Sydney marveled at the facility. On all sides of them were tanks, with oil flowing from one to the next. She was reminded again of the scope of the Prudhoe Bay operation. If anything happened here the loss would be catastrophic. They passed a couple of crew members at their work stations along the way, but no one tried to stop them or question their presence.

The monitoring station should have been manned at all times. But when they arrived, they found it was deserted.

"Shotgun, we have a problem," Jack said.

CHAPTER 12

"There isn't anyone at the monitoring station," Jack said through his comm.

"Copy that, Raptor," Vaughn replied. His voice was low, almost a whisper. "They're all over here."

Sydney and Jack broke into a run, heading for the pump station. There was no question of keeping a low profile now.

The two agents sprinted between two towering fuel tanks and around the humming auxiliary generator that powered the pumps. They stopped at the edge of the generator, and Sydney took a small reflector from her pocket. Angling the surface around the corner, she took in the scene at the pig launching facility. She saw that there were five men at the launch site, standing around the access hatch. Two of them, shielded behind the other three, held what looked like a cleaning pig.

One of the men holding the object was Rod Chambers.

So it's a perfectly innocent maintenance procedure, Sydney thought. *Except that there's no scheduled cleaning and the pig would not be expected at either of the two normal retrieval sites—Pump Station Four or the Valdez Marine Terminal—if it even made it that far. And it doesn't take five men to launch a pig.*

"This is Phoenix. We're in position. I see five men at the pig launch site. How about you, Shotgun?"

"Roger that. Five *big* men," Vaughn said. "At least they aren't expecting us."

"Don't be too sure, Shotgun," Jack said. "If they were at all suspicious of me, they may expect someone to try to stop them." He quickly issued assignments. "Shotgun, you lead. I'll be two seconds behind you. Evergreen, you back up Shotgun. Phoenix"—he glanced at Sydney as he stepped in front of her—"give me a few seconds, then you're on Chambers. Our primary objective is to stop that supposed pig from launching. Everything else is secondary."

Jack hesitated for a few seconds as each of the agents drew a deep breath and prepared to sprint into action.

At the launch site Chambers and his helper, a muscled blond with chiseled Nordic features, set the pig down. Each man took out a small wrench and began to remove the bolts securing the access hatch.

"Now!" Jack said into his comm.

At Jack's signal Vaughn burst from behind the north wall, where he had been crouched, waiting. His movement caught the attention of the men.

"Stop him, George!" Chambers yelled.

The man closest to Vaughn, a solidly built African American with tightly braided cornrows covering his head, moved toward Vaughn.

On the south side Jack made his move. He emerged from his hiding place behind the generator and headed for Rod Chambers.

Chambers spotted him. His eyes flashed with recognition.

"Francis!" he yelled.

Jack's path was immediately blocked by another member of Chambers's crew, a broad Native American with a long black braid and dark eyes. The man lunged at Jack, grabbing him by one arm and spinning him around.

The fifth man, a duplicate of Chambers's Nordic assistant, moved back, helping his twin shield Chambers as he continued to work on the access hatch.

George moved closer to Vaughn. He reached out with one massive arm and caught Vaughn with a staggering backhanded blow to the side of the head.

Nadia ran from her cover to back up Vaughn. She caught him as he staggered backward, helping him stay on his feet.

As Vaughn regained his balance, Nadia continued toward George, feinting toward his right. She moved left as he swung again, then ducked under his moving arm, bringing the heel of her hand up against the big man's chin. His jaw snapped shut with a sickening crunch of tooth against tooth, and she moved past him.

Francis continued to swing Jack around until

he was facing back the way he'd come, using Jack's own momentum to drive him away from Chambers. Jack didn't fight the movement. Rather, he allowed himself to be spun around, then continued the rotation, turning the inertial force against his attacker.

Francis was short and stocky, and he proved harder to move than Jack had anticipated. Initially caught off balance, Francis spun for a few steps, then stopped, slowing Jack and putting a stop to their insane dance.

George, meanwhile, had recovered from the blow to his jaw. Nadia had run past him, but he was on her in two long strides. Coming up behind her, George wrapped his massive arms around Nadia's waist, dragging her off her feet.

A few yards away Jack wrestled with Francis. Although Jack was quicker and more experienced, Francis was bigger and younger. His size alone presented Jack with a formidable obstacle to reaching Chambers.

Chambers dug at the bolts on the access hatch. His blond companion had removed one bolt before the APO team had attacked, and Chambers now had two more free. That left five bolts to go.

Chambers glanced over his shoulder at Jack. Francis still blocked the agent's path, a man-mountain in Jack's way. Chambers jerked his wrench, loosening another bolt. He snapped a socket over the loose bolt and ratcheted it off. Four more bolts to go.

Sydney moved out from behind the generator and sprinted toward Chambers and his twin guards. The split second of distraction she provided was all that Vaughn needed. He pulled a taser stick from a loop at his waist and shocked George in the back of the neck, afraid it would not penetrate the heavy clothing that covered the rest of the thug's body. The big man shook as the shock raced through his body. He lost his grip on Nadia.

Recovering quickly, George whirled to confront the source of his pain. He swung his beefy left forearm at Vaughn, knocking the taser wand away. It clattered across the concrete floor and landed against the base of the generator.

Chambers dropped another bolt on the floor. He had three left.

Jack charged Francis. His height gave him an advantage in the rush, and the two men crashed to the floor in front of Sydney. Without missing a step she jumped, landing with one foot squarely in the middle of Francis's back, putting him out of commission. Sydney spun around and faced one of the blond twins.

On the other side of the fracas, Vaughn shouted to Nadia to go back Sydney up.

Nadia moved in to confront the other twin, leaving Vaughn to struggle with George.

Behind the twins Chambers spun another bolt loose. He had only two more left.

Sydney sized up the blond in front of her. Tall and well muscled, he looked like an Alpine ski champion. She could glimpse Chambers behind him, working furiously on the next-to-last bolt. She had to get past the blond. The primary objective was the pig. The men were merely obstacles to overcome.

Nadia had retrieved Vaughn's taser, and Sydney pulled a fighting stick from her waistband. They couldn't risk gunfire inside the facility. Instead, they both had weapons that required them to get close to their opponents.

"Hans! Lars!" Chambers's voice commanded the twins. "I need another minute."

Sydney caught her sister's eye for an instant.

The two women nodded, and attacked simultaneously, before Hans and Lars could go on the offensive. Sydney took two running steps toward Lars—or was it Hans? She gauged his height and spun into the air, lashing out with the side of one foot. The kick caught him square in the face. There was a moment of resistance, then she felt his nose yield to the impact.

He couldn't control the instinctive reaction, and his hands flew to his damaged face. He roared in pain and charged at Sydney.

Nadia moved with the grace of a dancer as she approached Hans—or was it Lars?—and then pulled back, just out of his reach as he lunged at her and moved away from Chambers, leaving an opening for Sydney to move in toward the target, if she could only get past Lars.

Jack grabbed the dark braid that hung down Francis's back. Using the braid as a handle, he yanked Francis's head up. He was rewarded with a painful-sounding crack from Francis's thick neck.

Francis wasn't defeated yet, however. He struggled to reach behind him as his body bucked in an effort to throw Jack from his back.

Jack yanked the braid sideways once again,

twisting the man's neck at an unnatural angle. Then he slammed his weight against the back of Francis's head, slamming his face against the floor. Still using the braid, he repeated the blow. Francis stopped struggling.

Vaughn tried to stay away from George's fists and arms. Staying low, he came in at a crouch under the tall man's reach.

Vaughn turned his right side toward George and balanced his weight on his left foot. Pushing off with his left leg, he drove his right foot into George's right knee. The blow landed to the side of his kneecap, pushing the bone aside and stretching the tendons and cartilage. The leg gave way and George dropped to his knees, landing painfully on the damaged joint.

Chambers threw a piece of hardware on the floor and turned his attention to the last bolt.

Nadia backed up a few inches, daring Hans to follow her. He accepted the challenge, stalking her as she drew slowly back, away from both Chambers and the fight between Vaughn and George. Nadia teased Hans with the taser gun, silently taunting him, tempting him to try to take it away from her.

Vaughn rose quickly from his crouch. He

yanked at his belt buckle, which broke away, producing a slender cord. At each end was a metal ring, which had been part of the buckle. He raced behind George, jumping the man from behind and throwing the cord over his head and around his neck. Vaughn drew the cord tight, shutting off the man's windpipe.

It would only take a little more pressure to crush George's throat.

Sydney dodged the charging Lars and moved closer to Chambers.

Nadia feinted at Hans with the taser gun. He blocked her thrust, grabbed the end of the weapon, and twisted, trying to wrest it from her grip. Nadia pirouetted with the wand, breaking his hold. The move left him open for a moment, and she took the opportunity, shoving the prongs against his chest.

The shock raced through Hans. He stopped, shaking as the current passed through him. Nadia pressed her advantage, sending jolt after jolt into him. He fell to the ground, and she twisted his arms behind him, tightening a plastic restraint around his wrists.

Meanwhile, Chambers pulled the last bolt from

the access hatch. He grabbed the handle on the steel plate and dropped the plate to the floor. There was a loud crash as metal met concrete.

Now he just had to load the pig into the chute.

Sydney was only a couple of steps away as Chambers struggled to lift the bulky pig by himself. She charged him, then stopped in her tracks when she heard Vaughn frantically yell her call sign.

She whirled around to see Lars, his nose still running with blood, his face red with rage. He was pointing an automatic at her.

She paused, gauging the distance between them. She might be able to disarm him before he could shoot her. Chambers was going to need help with the pig. If she could take out Lars, they could still stop Chambers.

Suddenly Lars pointed the gun away from her, toward the end of the massive fuel tank extending beyond the end of the generator.

"Phoenix! We can't let him shoot!" Jack yelled.

For what seemed like the hundredth time, Sydney regretted that they couldn't risk weapons fire in the facility.

She forced herself to relax and pull back from her attack posture. Even if he didn't hit the tank, there were too many other vulnerable places he *could* hit.

The pig was their primary objective, but their mission was to prevent damage to the pipeline and the rig. The safety of the facility had to come first.

Lars walked in a wide circle around Sydney, holding the gun steady and pointed in her direction. He wiped the blood from his face with his sleeve. His rage had cooled, replaced by an icy menace. Sydney had no doubt he would carry out his threat, even at the risk of himself and his team.

Lars could see the appraisal in her eyes. "Yes, Phoenix," he said, using the name he had heard Jack use. "You can't risk a shot in here."

Jack knelt over the limp form of Francis, still clutching the braid in his fist.

Vaughn held the cord taut against George's neck.

Nadia held Hans down, his hands behind his back.

Chambers continued struggling with the pig.

And Lars continued circling, out of reach of anyone on the APO team.

The cell phone link to headquarters squawked

in Sydney's ear as Dixon and Marshall asked for an update on the situation.

Sydney spoke to Lars, knowing Dixon and Marshall would hear her. "You might escape, but you can't be sure. You don't know what damage a bullet would do in here."

"You don't think we planned for that? You underestimate us, Phoenix," Lars said. He moved closer to Chambers, who had managed to raise the pig a few inches off the floor. "We know very well what damage a bullet would cause. And so do you. You don't want to risk the destruction of the entire facility, do you?"

Sydney hesitated.

Lars took her reluctance for acquiescence. He waved toward Nadia. "Tell her to release my brother."

Sydney nodded to her sister.

Nadia set her mouth in a grim line. With elaborate slowness she rose from her position. The blond climbed to his feet with surprising agility, even though his hands were still restrained.

"Hans," his brother commanded, "give Chambers a hand with the robot."

For the moment Lars appeared to be in charge.

Hans moved the few steps to the hatch, where

Chambers lowered the pig and undid the restraints on the man's wrists.

His back to Lars, Vaughn still crouched over George, slowly tightening the cord around the big man's neck. His movements were shielded by his body, and Lars's attention was on Sydney. The cord was so tight George couldn't make a sound. Vaughn could feel the tension of the cord as it dug into the flesh of George's neck. There was only one way he could think of to create a distraction and give Sydney an opening.

Slowly Vaughn loosened the cord.

He felt it give against George's flesh, and heard George's strangled cry. The man bucked beneath him, trying to free himself. Vaughn fought to maintain control.

Lars glanced toward the source of the noise, his attention wavering for an instant. Instinctively his gun barrel followed his gaze.

At that moment Hans and Chambers were lifting the pig. Jack had subdued Francis, and Vaughn had George restrained.

Lars was alone. Sydney sprang at him.

Nadia lunged at Chambers, trying to prevent him from lifting the pig into the pipe.

198

Lars recovered, and Sydney found herself looking down the barrel of his gun. She could see his finger tightening on the trigger as he pulled back.

Suddenly someone pushed her to the ground from behind. She heard the crack as the gun fired, and felt a searing pain burn through her left thigh. Her leg felt as if it were on fire. Jack threw himself on top of her, shielding her from the possibility of another shot.

Chambers and Hans were holding the pig about three feet above the floor. They swung it back, in time to catch Nadia in the midsection with the heavy mechanism. She collapsed on the floor, temporarily unable to breathe.

Hans and Chambers quickly shoved the pig into the intake shunt and turned the valves that released it into the pipeline.

"Done!" Chambers yelled in triumph. "Let's go!"

Chambers, Hans, and Lars ran for the north exit. They didn't bother to give a second glance to the downed members of their team.

Seconds later they were gone.

And the pig was starting its journey down the pipeline.

CHAPTER 13

Jack grabbed Sydney's cell phone link and shouted to Marshall and Dixon back in Los Angeles. "Phoenix is down! She took a bullet!"

Jack knelt next to Sydney and carefully began to examine her, looking for injuries.

Nadia climbed to her feet and shuffled toward her sister. She was still doubled over and could barely walk, but her concern for Sydney overrode her own pain.

Vaughn reached into his coat pocket and withdrew a hypodermic needle. He injected George with a short-term tranquilizer, then released the pressure on his neck. The big man went slack.

The two men Chambers had left behind were in custody and completely immobilized. Now Vaughn had a mission to complete.

"Raptor," Dixon said over the cell link, "this is Outrigger. We will send a medical team, but we need to know how serious the wound is."

"I'm checking now," Jack replied, continuing his examination. He could still hear her scream of pain in his ears.

Jack rolled Sydney onto her side, revealing a small pool of blood that was growing underneath her. Without waiting for him to ask, Sydney set her jaw against the pain and tried to move her injured leg. White-hot pain lanced through her thigh, but she was able to move.

"Nothing's broken," she gasped. "But it hurts like hell."

Jack probed the wound, checking the rate at which she was losing blood.

"Outrigger, there are no broken bones, and the bullet appears to have missed the major arteries. But she needs medical attention," Jack informed Dixon.

"Roger that, Raptor. We'll get a rig medic over there as fast as we can," Dixon said.

Nadia sat down next to Sydney and cradled her sister's head in her lap. She motioned to Jack to help Vaughn. Jack nodded and moved away.

Jack and Vaughn quickly trussed up the two injured thugs. They were both unconscious, and therefore unable to give the two agents any information. But there was only one place the pig could have gone. It was in the pipeline and headed for Valdez, with a disaster planned along the way. A disaster they had to avert.

"How is she?" Vaughn asked Jack as they worked.

Jack grunted as he pulled a restraint tight. "She'll live. There's no arterial bleeding, no broken bones. I just don't want her to move right now."

Vaughn nodded, tight-lipped. He wanted to run over to Sydney and see for himself that she would be all right. But what he wanted didn't matter right now—all that mattered was the mission.

"Merlin," Jack addressed Marshall back at headquarters, "can you track that pig they put in the pipeline?"

"Affirmative, Raptor. The marine terminal at

Valdez has monitors all over the pipeline. We're tapped into their feed through a series of satellite uplinks that are designed to—"

"Then the answer is yes," Jack interrupted.

"Uh, yeah," Marshall replied.

"Good. Tell us where it is," Jack said.

"It is . . ." Marshall paused for a moment while he analyzed the feed. "It is two miles down the line."

"Roger that," Jack said. He turned to Vaughn. "Two miles. Are you ready?"

Vaughn shot a glance at Sydney. Nadia was hunched over her, stroking her hair and trying to make her as comfortable as possible while they waited for the medic to arrive.

Vaughn pushed away the desire to go to Sydney's side, and nodded to Jack. He grabbed the tools Chambers had abandoned, adding them to the assortment already in his pockets.

Jack cocked an eyebrow at him.

Vaughn shrugged. "They might come in handy."

"You could be right," Jack said.

"Evergreen!" Vaughn's voice pulled Nadia's attention away from her sister. Her head came up, and she looked at Vaughn. "Get whatever you can from these guys when they wake up," he said. "Do whatever it takes. Raptor and I are going after the pig."

"I will," she said. Then she turned her attention back to her sister. Until the prisoners were alert enough to question, Sydney was her priority.

Jack headed back the way he had come, Vaughn at his heels.

None of the regular crew members on the rig had heard the gunshot. The noise of the rig, and their ear protectors, had muffled the sound. As Jack and Vaughn moved away from the deserted control console and back across the main production floor, they saw with relief that the operation appeared to be running normally. No one knew they might be only minutes from disaster.

When they reached the parking lot, Jack led the way to the pickup he had driven earlier. He started the engine, and they were on their way.

"Merlin," Jack said as he drove along the gravel road leaving the rig, "give me some direction."

"Roger, Raptor. Give me a sec," Marshall replied.

Both men knew the feed was going to Nadia

and Sydney as well. The two female agents could hear everything Jack and Vaughn said, although Jack was now the only one with a connection to headquarters.

"Raptor, this is Outrigger. We have a medic on the way to Phoenix and Evergreen, along with a couple of security people. They should be there in a minute or two."

"Thanks, Outrigger. Does Merlin have those directions yet?" Jack asked.

"Just stick to the highway for now, Raptor, and make up as much speed as possible. We'll get back to you," Dixon replied.

Jack glanced over at Vaughn. "Hang on."

Jack pounded the accelerator, and the truck fishtailed slightly before picking up speed. They were past Deadhorse now, headed down the Dalton Highway. The headlights cut through the black night.

Jack repeated what Dixon had said about the medic, for the benefit of the rest of the team.

"Shouldn't we be heading for the pipeline?" Vaughn asked.

"Outrigger says to stay on the highway and move as fast as we can," Jack replied. He slid the truck through a turn, the wheels spinning for a moment in the snow, then regaining traction. "On this road, that shouldn't be over about fifteen miles per hour," Jack continued. "But Merlin assured me this vehicle was set up for these road conditions. He swears it will do at least thirty without any trouble, even in the snow."

Jack's words didn't reassure Vaughn. Outside the night was pitch dark, with the only light coming from their high-powered headlights and the eerie reflection of the moonlight on the snow.

"The road parallels the pipeline," Jack said. "We won't be very far from it."

"Do you know this road?" Vaughn asked.

"I drove part of it this afternoon, and I studied the map for a bit," Jack replied.

Which means you committed the road to memory, and checked out the truck, Vaughn thought. He relaxed a fraction. *Jack knows what he's doing. At least when it comes to his assignment.*

"Evergreen," Vaughn said over the comm, "is the medic there yet?"

"Affirmative, Shotgun," Nadia said. Her voice was reassuring. "They're taking her out on a stretcher, but they tell me it's only a flesh wound. She'll be fine."

"Thanks," Vaughn said, his voice husky.

Jack shot him a hard look but immediately returned his attention to the road as they continued to fly down the darkened highway.

Sydney bit her lip against the pain as the medics lifted her onto the stretcher. Nadia was beside her, holding her hand and offering her comfort.

Two rig security guards were helping the now-conscious George to his feet and escorting him out of the building.

"I have to go," Nadia said, glancing toward George.

Sydney nodded. She understood the importance of the mission and Nadia's part in it. She squeezed her sister's hand. "I'm fine," she said unconvincingly.

"I'll be back as soon as I can," Nadia promised.

Sydney watched her sister follow the security guards from the building. Nadia would get whatever information George had to offer, she was sure of that.

Sydney listened as her father relayed instructions from Dixon. She clenched and unclenched her fists in frustration. She should be in the truck with her father, not lying on a stretcher.

The medics moved rapidly, carrying her from the production facility to a medical unit at one end of the building. There, a young doctor quickly cleaned and stitched her wound. When she tried to get up to go find Nadia, he refused to let her move.

"You need time to heal," he said, pushing her back down on the cot.

Sydney noted the man's patronizing tone and bit back a sharp retort. This was someone used to giving orders and used to having them obeyed.

She knew how to deal with men like that. Her father, and Arvin Sloane, had taught her well.

Nadia watched her prisoner from outside the two adjoining cells that constituted the Deadhorse jail. Normally used to house oil riggers whose disputes had progressed past scuffling and threats, the facility wasn't designed for interrogation. Still, she had worked with a lot less and enjoyed successful results.

"So, George," Nadia began. She paced back and forth, her arms crossed over her chest. "You don't mind if I call you George, do you?" She paused and stared at the big man. He glared back at her, refusing to answer. She shrugged. "George it is, then," she said.

Still no answer.

"I suppose I could call you Mr. Carver, if you'd prefer," Nadia went on.

The man's head shot up at the mention of his surname. He seemed surprised.

"Oh, I have my sources, George," Nadia said condescendingly. "George Carver was a great man. A role model for African Americans." She turned away from him, seeming to stare out a small window at the black night. "Your father must have had high hopes for you when he gave you that name."

Nadia watched George's reflection in the window. He didn't speak, but she could see her barb had hit its target. Anger flashed across his face for an instant, before he forced his expression into careful neutrality.

"George," she said, turning back around, "there are things I need to know. Things you need to tell me. Things that you will *want* to tell me."

She stopped, to let the implication of her words sink in.

"They left you, you know. Chambers and his blond friends. They abandoned you and Francis, and ran," Nadia said.

She held her hand to her ear, as though listening for a moment to a transmission from her fellow agents. She turned away slightly, making sure George could see the earpiece.

A slow smile spread across her face but didn't touch her eyes. "I don't think they will be coming back for you either. Not based on the reports I'm getting."

George rose from the narrow bunk where he had been sitting, and approached the bars of the cell. "They will," he said adamantly. But his voice was nowhere near as certain as his words.

Nadia shook her head and walked away. "No. They won't. Believe me."

She let the silence drag on. She had planted the seed of doubt in George's mind. She couldn't rush, though every second that passed brought them one second closer to disaster if she didn't get the essential intel from her captive.

"So. He is not coming back for you," she said. She waved one hand, as though dismissing the subject of Chambers. "You need to decide what you are going to do, George. Oh, you're going to jail, of course. That isn't the question. The question is where you will go to jail, and for how long."

Nadia walked to the door that led into the adjacent office. She swung the door open and looked back at George. "And you don't have much time."

The door shut behind her.

One of the security guards was waiting in the office. "Your sister is resting comfortably," he told her. "My partner is with the other prisoner, in the infirmary."

"Good," Nadia said.

She quickly procured a tray with two cups of hot coffee. Then she stuck the taser gun in her belt. Carrot and stick. She would use whichever she needed.

Sydney sat up on the hard infirmary cot. She reached for the glass of water on the table next to her and took a tentative sip. She was still a little shaky due to the blood loss, but she was getting stronger by the minute.

On the other side of the room the doctor was working on another patient, with a security guard standing close by. The body on the cot was obscured by a partially drawn curtain, but she could see enough to know it must be Francis. He didn't move, but an occasional groan escaped his lips as the doctor tended to his wounds.

She slid herself to the edge of the cot. As she swung her legs over the side, she felt the stitches pull. The pain was bearable. She sat for a minute, her legs dangling, then she stood up, putting her weight on her uninjured right leg.

Her clothes were at the foot of the cot, tossed on a chipped metal folding chair. She hobbled over, using the cot for support, and began rifling through her things.

She found her earpiece in the pocket of her coat, where she had hidden it. Sloane had assured her, through her father, that the doctor and the security guards could be trusted. Still, she had seen no reason to take chances—at least not until she could be sure she was firmly in control. She replaced the receiver in her ear and tested the transmitter. "Raptor, this is Phoenix."

Vaughn's voice came through her receiver. "Good to hear you, Phoenix," he said, relief evident in his tone. "Raptor is on the link to headquarters. What's your status?"

Sydney felt an instant warmth when she heard Vaughn's voice. There was still so much that seemed unsettled between them.

"A few stitches, Shotgun. Not much else." She glanced across the room to where the doctor continued working. He appeared to be ignoring her.

"The doctor is working on one prisoner, and Evergreen is with the other. One of the security guards is on each of them."

"Roger that, Phoenix. Glad to hear you're okay," Vaughn said.

Vaughn glanced over at Jack, who was deep in conversation with Dixon and Marshall. Jack nodded, indicating he had heard Sydney's report, and passed the information along to headquarters. A minute later he raised his voice and addressed Vaughn, knowing the rest of the team would be listening. "They're tracking the pig. It's moving pretty fast, but we should be able to get ahead of it."

They reached the summit of a short rise and headed down a long hill. Vaughn could see the pipeline off to the right, a pale outline in the moonlight. It zigzagged along its path a few yards from the road. Jack had been correct; they were not very far from the line.

"Then what?" Vaughn asked.

"There's an access port at the pump station," Jack said. "We have to get there first and get the pig out of the line. If it gets that far."

* * *

214

Nadia listened as George told his story. He had accepted the cup of steaming coffee—*and* the promise of help with his sentencing.

So far she hadn't needed to use the taser. But she was ready to if necessary.

"He didn't tell me much. He said nobody would know nothin' before we were long gone," George was saying.

"Gone?" she asked. "How?"

"He said there would be a plane coming in tonight. Told me his boss would send it for us. All we had to do was run that cleaning pig through the line."

Nadia didn't challenge the obvious lie. Of course he knew it wasn't a cleaning pig, and he knew that she knew. But she let it pass. There would be time to dwell on that later.

"Go on," she said.

"That was it," George said. He shrugged. "We're gonna put the pig in the line, get on the plane at midnight, and be gone before anyone notices anything."

Nadia stood up. "Give me a minute," she said.

From the office she contacted Jack on her comm.

"Raptor, this is Evergreen. Our subject claims that his team is leaving on a private plane at midnight. He says he was told no one would notice anything out of the ordinary before then."

Jack relayed the information to Dixon and Marshall, and listened for their reply.

"We will try to verify that, Evergreen," Dixon said.

"Okay. I better get back in there," Nadia said. She picked up the coffeepot and carried it back to the cell with her. She would keep pouring as long as George kept talking.

Jack pulled the cell phone headset from his ear. "Dixon and Marshall are working on a solution, but I need to concentrate on the road. You take this," he said, tossing the headset to Vaughn.

"Outrigger, this is Shotgun. What is our status?" Vaughn asked.

"We're picking up the trackers on both you and the device. It's still ahead of you, but not far," Dixon replied.

"I want to send Evergreen and Phoenix to the airport," Vaughn said.

Jack glanced over, his eyes narrowed. Vaughn ignored him. Sloane's voice came over the line. He sounded distant, and Vaughn realized he must be on a speaker phone in Marshall's lab. "Do you really think that's wise?" Sloane asked.

"Yes, I do." Vaughn's reply was firm. "Three members of that team are still at large. The incoming aircraft is their only quick way out of here. If we want to take them, Evergreen and Phoenix are our best bet."

"Understood," Sloane said. His voice betrayed no emotion. Like Jack, he did not let personal feelings interfere with his job. That Nadia was his daughter simply did not enter into his decision. She was the right person for the task.

Still, as Vaughn issued his orders, pulling Nadia from her interrogation and ordering Sydney from the infirmary—over the protests of the doctor—he was reminded that Jack *had* allowed his personal feelings to affect him. He had protected Sydney during the altercation at the rig.

Vaughn was sure Jack would claim he was protecting a member of the team. But Vaughn knew better—Jack was protecting his daughter. Jack had allowed himself to be a father first, if only for a split second, and it had saved Sydney's life. Vaughn turned back to Jack. He expected an argument, but

Jack's lips were clamped in a thin line and he was focused on the road ahead of him.

The headlights formed a bright tunnel through the night. On either side of the road, moonlight washed the snow in a faint glow that exaggerated shadows and obscured the landscape.

The link to headquarters had gone silent after Vaughn's exchange with Sloane. Now it came to life again, with Marshall at the other end.

"Shotgun, this is Merlin," Marshall said.

"Merlin, what do you have for me?" Vaughn asked.

"We're tracking the device, and it looks like you're about even with it. The pipeline doesn't go in a straight line, so that when it expands and contracts with the heat and cold, it has some give. Ingenious design, really, when you consider the extreme weather, and the length of the line—" Vaughn heard Dixon's whispered interruption pull Marshall back from his digression.

"Anyway," Marshall continued, "you should be ahead of the pig within the next few minutes, and at your present speed your lead will continue to grow."

"Then why don't we just stop and get the

damned thing out?" Vaughn asked. He was frustrated with the delay. Every minute they waited was another minute closer to whatever Chambers and his boss, Soukis, had planned. Another minute closer to an ecological and financial disaster.

"There are only a few places along the line where you can get inside the pipe without causing major damage," Marshall explained.

Vaughn grunted.

"One of those places is at the pump station, and that's about thirty miles from Deadhorse. At the rate you're moving, you should reach Pump Station One in approximately thirty-one minutes and twenty-four seconds." Marshall clicked a few keys, and Vaughn could picture him tapping at his computer keyboard. "That is, of course, if you maintain your current speed, which you should be quite able to do."

"And there isn't anywhere closer that we can do this?" Vaughn asked, still anxious.

"Negative, Shotgun. Not unless you want to cause as much damage as we are trying to prevent. Pump Station One," Marshall replied.

CHAPTER 14

OIL RIG INFIRMARY
DEADHORSE, ALASKA

Sydney clamped her teeth down on her lip as she pulled her jeans over her legs. The stiff fabric rubbed against her wound, even through the bandage and her heavy cotton long johns, and sent streaks of pain along her leg.

She forced herself to remain silent. If the doctor heard her, he would definitely check on her, and if he did he would insist on keeping her in the infirmary. And she had no intention of staying. She didn't want to waste time arguing with him or having to ask Dixon to go over the doctor's head. That was time they didn't have.

With Nadia's help, she was able to dress quickly. She was thankful that Nadia had brought her a change of clothes—her high-tech snowsuit had been cut away by the doctor. At least she still had her parka and her boots.

She tucked in her shirt and buttoned her jeans. She had to lean on Nadia to put on her right boot. Her left leg wouldn't be able to support her entire weight for a few more days at least.

But as long as she had both legs firmly planted on the ground, she'd be fine.

Silently the two women moved toward the door. A few more feet, and they would be out of the infirmary.

From the other end of the room came a loud groan and some muffled curses. Sydney was curious about Francis, but not enough to delay her exit. She took advantage of the distraction and slipped through the door, with Nadia right behind her.

They made their way down the corridor of the medical facility. Sydney fastened her parka and pulled on her gloves. Fortunately, aside from the doctor cutting away her snowsuit, the rest of her gear was intact and exactly as she'd left it.

Nadia took a gun from her coat and handed it to Sydney. They had just stepped outside, which meant that they could risk gunfire if they had to.

They moved swiftly across the snow to Nadia and Vaughn's vehicle—another beat-up pickup truck. They hopped in and drove around the lake to the deserted airfield.

The landing lights glowed softly, outlining the runway. Although there was no operator on duty, the lights remained on from dusk until dawn.

Sydney and Nadia had no idea where Chambers and the twins had gone when they fled the facility. They'd had plenty of time to hide themselves while they waited for their plane to arrive, but there was only one place to land a plane in Deadhorse. Chambers would have to come to them.

Syd and Nadia would have to wait him out in the subzero temperatures.

Nadia was prepared for the weather. On the floor of the cab was a miniature high-efficiency oil burner. They wouldn't be toasty—no heater could hold back the extreme cold that surrounded them—but it would keep them safe from frostbite and hypothermia for the next few hours. Nadia lit the burner and slid down in her seat until only the top of her head was visible through the window. She spread a quilt over her body and tucked it under her chin, gesturing for Sydney to do the same.

The thickly insulated blanket not only trapped the heat from the heater, but it also shielded the glow of the burner. From the outside the truck would look deserted.

DALTON HIGHWAY
20 MILES SOUTH OF DEADHORSE

Jack kept his eyes on the road. At this speed, in the snow, he couldn't afford to lose his concentration. Beside him Vaughn handled the radio traffic, relaying information between Nadia and Sydney at the airport and Marshall, Dixon, and Sloane in Los Angeles.

Jack made some quick mental calculations. "Another twenty-five minutes, maybe thirty," he said.

Vaughn nodded, listening to a report coming through from Dixon. "Roger that, Outrigger," he said. He turned to Jack and spoke to the team. "Evergreen. Phoenix. Merlin advises there is an aircraft approaching Deadhorse. Outrigger wants to know as soon as you see it."

Jack cleared his throat. "Does headquarters know anything about the flight?"

"Not much," Vaughn replied. "It originated in Seattle and it's a small jet. The registration is buried in layers of corporate ownership."

Jack shook his head and kept his eyes on the road. "So we don't know who's on board."

"They're working on that," Vaughn said. "They have people on the ground in Seattle checking with the service crew there. Merlin said he would have an answer soon."

"Raptor. Shotgun. This is Phoenix. We have visual confirmation of the flight," Sydney announced.

"Roger that, Phoenix," Vaughn replied, then relayed the information to Dixon. "Phoenix reports visual confirmation of the flight."

"Tell her to hang on, Shotgun. We should have intel on that flight in another couple of minutes," Dixon said. Vaughn could hear him turn and talk to someone else in the room, then he came back on the link. "Ask Phoenix how soon she thinks the flight will be on the ground."

"Phoenix, how much time until touchdown?" Vaughn asked.

"I'm not sure," Sydney said. "They're still a

few minutes out. We can see their lights, and they are definitely headed this way. My best guess is no more than five or six minutes."

"Any sign of our friends from the rig?" Vaughn asked.

"Negative on that, Shotgun. Very quiet here, for now," Sydney said.

It was quiet in the moving truck too. Jack kept his speed up, pushing the limits of the vehicle and his skill behind the wheel. The truck bounced and slid on the slippery surface, which consisted of gravel and new snow. But they managed to stay on the road. Every second was precious, especially now that the plane was descending into Deadhorse. Once the conspirators were safely in the air, anything might happen.

"Do you think it's possible," Jack began slowly, "that Chambers has a dead-man switch on the pig? That he might detonate it if he's attacked?"

Vaughn considered the possibility. "What's stopping him from detonating it now? He'll be in the air in a few minutes, or at least he expects to be. Why not finish the job, if he can?" he asked.

"Shotgun, this is Merlin. I think I can answer that for you," Marshall offered.

"Go ahead, Merlin," Vaughn said, letting the others know he was listening to Marshall on the cell link.

"From our analysis it looks like the most trouble would be done by attacking an underground segment of the pipe. The aboveground stretches might sustain more direct damage, but they're also easier and faster to repair," Marshall said.

The sinking feeling in Vaughn's stomach told him Marshall was right. The pipeline was buried many feet below the surface, encased in insulating material. In some spots it was even refrigerated to prevent the heat of the moving oil from damaging the permafrost. A break in one of those areas would be difficult, expensive, and time-consuming to repair.

"Merlin, tell me there isn't one of those stretches between here and Pump Station One," Vaughn said.

"Negative on that, Shotgun. There isn't an area for them to target before you get to Pump Station One. Actually"—Marshall stopped for a minute, clicked some keys, and resumed—"you should reach station one in approximately twenty minutes and six seconds. Give or take a few seconds."

"Thanks, Merlin," Vaughn said. He took a minute to explain Marshall's theory to the rest of the team. It made sense, but it didn't put his mind at ease. So far nothing about this mission had been smooth. They had followed so many different leads, only to find dead ends. They had been a step or two behind Soukis and his employees ever since the first hint of trouble on the Petroleum Associates drilling platform.

DEADHORSE AIRPORT
DEADHORSE, ALASKA

Sydney leaned forward in her seat as the small jet touched down. She was grateful for her layers of clothing, despite the pain it took to get them on; it had gotten quite cold in the vehicle. Nadia had extinguished the oil heater, and the temperature in the truck cab was dropping quickly. She had also disabled the interior lights, so the illumination wouldn't give them away when they opened the doors.

Sydney put her hand in her pocket and wrapped her fingers around the automatic Nadia had given her. Lars hadn't hesitated to shoot her. Now she might return the favor. In any case, she was not going to let the men get on that plane.

The high-pitched whine of jet engines echoed across the empty airport as the pilot reversed the thrust. The plane slowed, the nose dropping slightly.

Sydney tensed, ready to move as soon as Chambers showed himself.

"Phoenix, Evergreen, this is Shotgun," Vaughn said.

"Go ahead," Sydney replied.

"Outrigger tells us that there are two people aboard that plane, according to the service crew in Seattle. The description of one fits the man who visited our friend Blake in the hospital. The other is a charter pilot, under contract to one of Mr. Soukis's transportation companies," Vaughn informed her.

"Roger that, Shotgun," Sydney said.

The plane rolled to a stop.

Nadia was already out of the truck, concealed behind the high front fender.

Sydney opened her door, the faint click of the latch lost in the scream of the two jet engines. She eased the door closed behind her and crouched against it, her silhouette absorbed in the larger bulk of the truck.

Snow had been cleared for the Alaska Airlines flight earlier in the day, and no new snow had fallen since. The sleek Cessna Citation sat idling on the tarmac, ready for the new passengers to board.

A door opened just behind the cockpit of the plane, and a set of steps folded out. From the far side of the runway three figures ran forward, illuminated by the landing lights along the ground. Sydney could identify each of them as they came closer.

Lars. Hans. And Chambers.

Sydney and Nadia had considered various scenarios while they waited. After all, their situation was not ideal. They were outnumbered, Sydney was injured, the other members of their team were miles away, and the already meager local security forces were stretched even thinner by the two men they had taken prisoner and had to guard. Their options were limited. They had only a sketchy plan: Keep the pilot and his sidekick on the plane, and keep Chambers and the twins off. Beyond that, they would have to improvise. But they were not without resources.

"Cover me," Nadia said. Her voice sounded confident, determined.

Sydney drew her weapon and trained her aim on the three men who were approaching the tarmac.

Nadia darted out from behind the fender, a small canister in her hand. Sydney saw her trigger the canister and roll it toward the open door of the plane.

Hans—or was it Lars?—spotted Nadia as she took cover around the corner of the closed terminal building.

Sydney could see the twin's mouth open in a shout, but it was drowned out by the continuing noise from the engines. The pilot was making no effort to shut them down. Sydney guessed he must not have planned to be on the ground for very long.

Beneath the steps of the plane a cloud of pale gray smoke rose from the tear gas canister that Nadia had released. The smoke billowed up, flowing through the open door of the plane. In response, as Sydney and Nadia had hoped, the door began to close against the noxious fumes. Chambers and the twins were locked outside, and they retreated rapidly from the cloud that wafted across the runway.

Sydney knew they had only bought a few minutes' time—Chambers and his crew wouldn't be stopped this easily. She reached one arm back into the cab of the truck and retrieved a small bag she had left on the seat. She stuffed it into her coat pocket and carefully loosened the drawstring on the bag. She reached gingerly inside and took out a collection of razor-sharp throwing stars—silent weapons that would not give away her presence.

Chambers and the twins had retreated to the far side of the runway. Sydney and Nadia had the advantage of being upwind of the tear gas, but it would dissipate soon.

DALTON HIGHWAY
25 MILES SOUTH OF DEADHORSE

Jack could feel his muscles beginning to tighten up. He had been clutching the steering wheel of the truck and driving as fast as humanly possible through dangerous road conditions for close to an hour.

A few more minutes and they would leave the highway. And then it would get worse.

"Shotgun, this is Merlin. We're still tracking

the pig. You're well ahead of it. There is an access road leaving the highway in six miles. It will take you to Pump Station One. We'll have more for you once you're there," Marshall said.

"Roger, Merlin," Vaughn replied. He turned to Jack. "Six miles to the turn. It shouldn't be long now."

Jack nodded his head.

Vaughn spoke into his comm. "Phoenix, are you there? What's your status?"

"This is Evergreen," Nadia's voice came back over the line. "We've stopped Chambers and his friends from getting on the plane, for now. They know I'm here, but they haven't spotted Phoenix yet. With luck, they will think she is still in the infirmary."

Which, thought Vaughn, was exactly where she should be. But she had a job to do, just as he did. There was no time for weakness.

"All right, Evergreen. We're nearly to the pump station turnoff. We only need about fifteen minutes. Do you think you can hold them off that long?" Vaughn asked.

"Yes," Sydney said firmly. "These guys are *not* getting away from us."

DEADHORSE AIRPORT
DEADHORSE, ALASKA

In the darkness beyond the runway lights, Sydney could see the three men moving. They separated, two going one way, one the other. They were closing in on Nadia in a classic flanking approach.

But they were moving toward a single target—they didn't know Sydney was there.

"Evergreen," she whispered, "they're looking for you. It looks like two of them are heading around the back of the terminal building, and one is coming around the front. He'll have to go past me."

"Roger, Phoenix," Nadia whispered back. "Can you stop him without the others knowing?"

"Yes," Sydney whispered, gripping one of the stars.

Sydney crouched next to the truck. Pain shot through her leg, and she fought to control the trembling that threatened her balance. She waited, watching.

The plane began to taxi, moving away from the cloud of tear gas. The moving Cessna created turbulence, sending the gas in all directions and scattering the cloud. With their cover gone the three men sprinted across the runway, resuming their pincer attack. They still did not know Sydney was there.

At the end of the runway the pilot turned and came back toward the terminal, the door now facing away from Sydney.

The twins had gone behind the building. Chambers moved across the front, past the truck where Sydney hid. His attention was focused on the corner of the building where Nadia had disappeared.

Sydney held her breath and forced her leg to stop trembling. She would only have one chance.

From the end of the building came a burst of gunfire. Chambers broke into a run, crossing within a few feet of Sydney without noticing her. As he passed, she sprang up. Her injured leg protested, pain lancing up and down from her bullet wound, but the leg held her weight. She was only a few steps behind him now and she gauged the distance, adjusting for the moving target, and launched her silent weapon. The star flew straight, catching Chambers in the back of his head, ripping through his ski cap, and lodging in his scalp.

He screamed in pain and whirled to face his attacker.

Behind him Sydney saw Nadia round the corner

of the building, followed by Hans and Lars.

Both men had guns drawn, but they hesitated when they saw Chambers in the line of fire.

Nadia ran, twisting and turning, evading the men who chased her. She had to buy Vaughn a few more minutes. But the exertion in the extreme cold would exhaust her quickly.

Chambers lunged at Sydney, roaring in anger. She managed to sidestep his charge, but she felt something give way in her thigh as she tore her stitches loose. She had no time to worry about that now.

Chambers dove at her again, and she moved away. With a bad leg, she couldn't hope to physically beat him. She thought about the automatic in her pocket, but Nadia was in the line of fire. Even an expert shot could hit the wrong target, and Sydney was not willing to risk it.

The plane began to taxi toward them. Chambers called the twins, alerting them to the moving Cessna.

Hans and Lars trapped Nadia between them, one of them landing a solid blow as she tried to twist out of reach.

Sydney's concentration was broken for a fraction

of a second as Nadia went down. It was all Chambers needed. He lashed out, landing a well-aimed kick against her injured leg, sending her to her knees, and forcing her to drop her gun. Chambers kicked it away.

The three men dashed in front of the plane. Below its belly Sydney could see the stairs on the far side, gliding a few inches off the tarmac.

The pilot slowed the plane down. Sydney could see each man's feet and legs as one by one they grabbed the moving stairway and clambered aboard the taxiing jet. Sydney struggled to her feet as the stairs disappeared.

The door was closing. They were getting away.

She could feel blood running down her leg as she limped back to the truck. She yanked open the driver's side door and pulled herself into the seat. The keys were in the ignition. As the engine roared to life, Nadia jumped into the passenger seat. Sydney swung the truck onto the runway, chasing the plane. She would shoot out the tires, even ram them, if she had to. Anything to prevent the plane from taking off.

Nadia rolled down the window on her side, leaning out with her automatic. She sprayed the back of the plane with bullets. The jet engines roared, sending a searing cloud of jet wash back at her. Nadia ducked back inside, shielding herself from the heat, but not before her gun was caught on the window frame and ripped from her hand. It was blown away in the blast of heat that washed over them.

Sydney stomped the gas pedal to the floor, trying to overtake the jet as it picked up speed down the runway. They gained a few feet, weaving to the left side of the plane. The tail boom loomed ahead of them.

They were out of time. The plane would be off the ground in another minute, and soon it would be outside U.S. airspace.

"Take the wheel!" Sydney yelled at Nadia.

Nadia grabbed the steering wheel and slid behind it as Sydney opened the driver's side door.

"Get as close as you can," she said. She braced herself in the doorway for a second, then threw her right leg over the side of the pickup bed. Sydney shoved off from the cab of the truck, heaved herself over into the bed, and crouched there for a moment. The truck rocked from side to side as the two women moved, but it held the road.

As they passed under the tail, Sydney spoke into her comm. "Evergreen, all I have left is a few stars. If you can get me close enough, maybe I can jam their control surfaces and stop them from taking off," Sydney said. "I just need a clear shot."

"I'll get you as close as I can," Nadia replied grimly.

The truck gained a few more feet. Sydney stood up, looking over the cab.

The nose of the pickup was only inches from the wing. Nadia was matching the speed of the plane, holding the distance steady.

It was now or never.

Sydney threw a star over the cab and into the wing. The razor-sharp teeth bit into the metal skin of the aircraft, a few inches from the joint that was her target. Sydney threw the rest of the stars, one after the other. The second landed harmlessly in the wing, but the third lodged itself directly in the joint, followed by two more. It was the best she could do.

Her leg was wet with blood, and she couldn't stand up any longer. She crumpled to the floor of the pickup bed.

"Evergreen, let's get out of here," she said.

The truck veered away from the speeding

plane, turning off the asphalt at a sharp angle, and braking to a sudden halt in the snow at the side of the runway.

Looking out over the tailgate, Sydney watched the jet point its nose toward the black night sky and lift off. She had failed. Chambers had escaped.

Nadia jumped out of the cab and scrambled over to the side of the pickup. She looked at Sydney, disappointment and concern furrowing her brow.

The little jet climbed quickly and banked to the west. The climb slowed as the pilot began to level off.

Suddenly the wings bobbled. The plane tilted to the right. For an instant it looked as though it were flying sideways, standing on one wing tip. Then it flipped upside down.

Seconds later the sleek little plane plowed into the earth nose-first. Sydney and Nadia sat in silence as they watched the fireball blossom over the wreckage.

"Phoenix!" Sydney's comm came alive. "What was that?" Vaughn shouted.

"What is your status?" her father demanded.

"Raptor, Shotgun, it's under control," Sydney said. "We just canceled Mr. Chambers's flight."

CHAPTER 15

Jack listened to Sydney's reassuring words, but he heard the fatigue and weakness in her voice.

She had done her job. Now he had to do his.

"Phoenix, did either of you see any sign of a dead-man switch? Was Chambers carrying anything in his hands?" Jack asked.

"He was carrying something, Raptor. We don't know what it was," Nadia replied for Sydney.

Vaughn immediately alerted headquarters. "Merlin, do we still have a track on the pig?"

Marshall didn't answer right away, and the

silence made Vaughn's heart race. Everything they had done—including Sydney's taking a bullet in the leg—was for nothing if Chambers's last act had been to activate the robot.

"Uh, just a minute, Shotgun. There's something . . ." Marshall trailed off.

Vaughn glanced in the side mirror. There was nothing to see. The silent landscape was bare.

Jack checked the odometer and eased off the throttle. According to Marshall's calculations he should turn off the highway in the next half mile.

"Shotgun, this is Merlin. You're five hundred yards away."

Vaughn repeated the information, and Jack dropped his speed further. After flying down the highway for so long, they were now slowed to a crawl. Vaughn thought he could walk faster than the truck was moving.

"How about the pig, Merlin?" Vaughn asked again.

"We're working on it, Shotgun. We're working on it," Marshall replied.

"There!" Vaughn pointed to a break in the banked snow on the left side of the road. A rutted trail wound away from the highway, disguised by a blanket of snow.

Jack braked and pulled the truck off the highway onto the access road. The truck fishtailed slightly on the curve, then regained traction and bounced down the track. The truck churned through the accumulated snowfall. Clearly, no one had been down the track since the snow had fallen.

The pump station was only a couple hundred yards from the highway.

Vaughn braced his arms against the dash as they continued to bounce along the track toward the building that held the station.

"We've got it, Shotgun!" Marshall's voice cracked with relief. "I think the station at Valdez was trying to shut us out, but I reacquired the signal by tuning the satellite to another frequency—"

"Thanks, Merlin." Vaughn cut him off. "We're at the pump station."

In one minute they were stopped next to the building and facing a locked door. In one-and-a-half minutes they were inside.

The building was like all the others in that remote section of Alaska: a prefab box built on a foundation, with no adornment and few concessions to creature comfort.

Vaughn and Jack ran their high-powered

flashlights over the interior of the building. The pumps were crowded onto the concrete floor. Cooling fins rose from the pipes, just as they did on the supports outside. The radiating heat kept the inside temperature tolerable.

Vaughn stripped off his gloves and began examining the various pumps and controls.

"Merlin," he said, "what am I looking for?"

"You need to shut off the pumps and stop the flow. Then you can manually pump the oil until the pig is at the access hatch. The pig should reach your location in about three minutes."

"Where is the shutoff, Merlin?" Vaughn asked.

"Give me a second, Shotgun. I'm pulling up the plans now. I just got access to the construction company's database," Marshall said.

Vaughn heard the rapid-fire of Marshall striking a keyboard, and then a triumphant "Yes!"

"I have it, Shotgun. North wall. About a third of the way from the west side. There's an emergency shutoff. It will stop everything," Marshall announced.

Vaughn raced for the wall, calling for Jack to follow him. He found a wheel marked MANUAL CUT-OFF. ALARM WILL SOUND THROUGHOUT SYSTEM.

"I found the wheel, Merlin," Vaughn said.

"Hold on! Hold on! There's a flow control. A wheel to the right of where you're standing. Use that. The manual cutoff will cause problems of its own," Marshall cautioned.

"Got it," Vaughn said as he grabbed the wheel and tried to turn it. It wouldn't move.

Jack saw he needed help and grabbed the other side of the wheel, and between the two of them they managed to make it budge.

It moved with agonizing slowness.

Vaughn could feel the seconds ticking away. The pig would be very close by now.

"That's good," Marshall said over the cell link. "The valve is too small for that pig to get through now. You have to get it out of the line before it does any more damage."

"Any more damage?" Vaughn asked.

"There's been a small pressure drop a couple of miles up the line," Marshall said. "It may be nothing. I shouldn't have said anything."

"So now what?" Vaughn said.

"You remember the access panel Chambers opened in Deadhorse?" Marshall asked.

"Affirmative," Vaughn replied.

"This one should be identical. All the stations are exactly alike. It makes maintenance easier. Not that anything is easy in that climate—but still, easier," Marshall said.

"Right." Vaughn repeated the information for Jack, and threaded his way between the pumps, looking for one with a bypass and a shunt.

Jack moved down a second row of pumps.

"It's there, Shotgun," Marshall reported. "The monitors show it at the pump station. Whatever was in that pig, it's at the station now."

Vaughn forced his breathing to remain steady. He had to find the access hatch and get that thing out of the pipeline.

"Here!" Jack said. With his flashlight he illuminated a pump at the end of a row. There, in the circle of light, was the bypass with an access plate identical to the one Chambers had removed.

The steel plate, and eight bolts, were all that stood between them and the elusive, tainted pig.

"We found the hatch, Merlin," Vaughn said.

"All right. Now do exactly as I tell you," Marshall replied.

Jack took Vaughn's flashlight and moved to one side, creating a double circle of light, with the hatch in the center. Vaughn waited for Marshall's instructions.

"There's a digital readout on the left. You see it?" Marshall asked.

"Affirmative," Vaughn said. "I'm looking at the digital readout."

"That's the flow meter. Watch for it to stop. That means the pig is in the line, blocking the flow. It should be any second now," Marshall said.

Vaughn hoped he was right. Marshall was a genius, but he was hundreds of miles away.

"Do we have any idea what this thing is supposed to do?" Vaughn asked, watching the meter roll over another click.

"We *think* it's mechanical. The damage in the Caribbean wasn't caused by an explosion. On the other hand, that was a test run," Marshall replied. Vaughn could almost hear Marshall shrug. The truth was, they really didn't know.

"The flow looks like it's stopped," Vaughn said. The meter hadn't moved for nearly a minute.

"Roger that. Now you need to close the main line and open the valve that leads to the access hatch. There's a control ring just to the left of the meter," Marshall said.

Vaughn filled Jack in on Marshall's instructions.

Jack played the flashlight beam over the pipe near the hatch, illuminating the control ring.

"Got it," Vaughn said.

"Ease that back until you see the flow meter register."

Vaughn turned the ring, feeling the valve slide open in response. In a few seconds the flow meter began to register. "It's moving," he announced.

"Watch for five clicks, then shut it down tight," Marshall said.

Vaughn counted under his breath. "One. Two. Three. Four. Five!"

He grabbed the ring and slammed it shut.

"How did Chambers ever get that thing in the line, if he had to do all this?" Vaughn wondered out loud. "He only had a couple of minutes before we found him."

"That's a normal insertion point. It's set up for launching pigs on a regular basis. This is an emergency hatch," Marshall said. He never could resist sharing information, whether it was needed or not. "Now, are you ready for the next step?"

"Yes. We're ready for the next step," Vaughn said, looking at Jack.

Marshall talked Vaughn through draining the line, as Vaughn repeated his words for Jack's benefit.

It was finally time to open the hatch.

Vaughn looked at it closely. The bolts were an unusual shape. And he had just the right tool in his pocket.

Vaughn pulled Chambers's wrench from his pocket and waved it in Jack's direction. "You never know," he said.

Vaughn spun the bolts and lifted the plate off the hatch, exposing the pipe within.

And the pig.

"I can see it, Merlin."

"Lift it out. Carefully," Marshall added hastily. "Get it out of the building."

Jack stowed the flashlights and helped Vaughn lift the pig from the pipe. It was slippery with crude oil, extremely heavy, and awkward to carry.

Jack walked backward, carrying his end toward the door. He felt his way along by rubbing his shoulder against the wall. Without a light it was the best guide he had.

The two agents emerged from the building into the black night. They stumbled through the snow, lugging their clumsy load, until they were about thirty yards from the station.

Carefully they lowered the pig onto the ground.

Vaughn described the object to Marshall. He had thought of it as a pig, and it *was* shaped like a common dumbbell-style pig. But that was where the similarity ended.

"I really want to get a good look at it," Marshall said. "Shotgun, is there any way you can bring it back here?"

Vaughn heard protests in the background.

"Absolutely not," Dixon interrupted Marshall. "Not in its present condition."

"I didn't mean on—no—not before—" Marshall sputtered to a stop. In his fascination with exotic machinery, he hadn't realized what he had said.

"Shotgun, I'd like to examine it," Marshall said, "after you have deactivated it."

"Glad to oblige," Vaughn said. "We'll bring it home just as soon as you tell me how to deactivate."

"What you described sounds a lot like the Riskarski cutting tool. It's designed to burrow into a tunnel, then deploy cutting blades that enlarge the tunnel. The blades are spring-loaded. Quite ingenious, actually. But I don't see how that applies here," Marshall said. "Let me think about this a minute."

"We don't have a minute," Vaughn said. He was almost shouting in frustration. "We don't know how long we have."

"All right," Marshall said, sounding flustered for a moment. Then he regained his confident tone. "Look for a lid, or a removable plate. Some way to get inside the device."

"There's a latch of some kind on one end," Vaughn said. "But it's recessed. There isn't any way to reach—"

Vaughn stopped suddenly and patted his pockets. He pulled out a long, slender rod with a seemingly random array of prongs on the end.

"I know how to open it," he said.

"Shotgun, I don't think—," Marshall began.

Too late.

Vaughn stuck the rod into the deep recess, wiggling and twisting until the prongs lined up and the rod slid into place with a positive click. The rod had become a hinge, revealing a door that had not been visible before.

Jack shined a flashlight in as Vaughn opened the door, exposing a hollow interior. Inside was a row of metal saw blades, attached to a battery-powered shaft.

Deployed, they would have ripped and shredded the interior of the pipe, wreaking havoc until the battery had been expended.

"I don't see any wires except the ones to the battery," Vaughn told Marshall.

"It doesn't mean they aren't there," Marshall replied. "We need to disable it."

Vaughn sighed. It all came down to this. Disconnecting a battery. He would soon find out if it was booby-trapped. Even if it was, the pipeline was safe. He had done his job.

Vaughn reached over and took one of the flashlights from Jack. "No need for both of us to be here," he said.

Jack started to speak, but Vaughn held up a hand. "If I'm wrong, just take care of Sydney."

Jack looked at him coldly. "I don't need you to remind me to do that."

"No. But I needed to say it. Now get back behind the truck," Vaughn said.

Jack went without another word.

Vaughn shone the flashlight on the interior of the pig. If he thought of it as a pig, it seemed safer somehow. Using a pair of narrow long-nose pliers from his pilfered tool supply, he reached into the cavity. He drew a deep, steadying breath, then let it out. He clamped the wire in the pliers, and tugged.

Nothing happened. No explosions. No gas cloud. No high-voltage zap. Nothing, except the wire separating from the battery.

Vaughn was sure the team could have heard his sigh of relief without a comm device as he exhaled and closed his eyes.

CHAPTER 16

APO HEADQUARTERS
LOS ANGELES

Sydney eased herself into a chair next to Dixon. She rested her cane against the edge of the conference table.

The doctor had insisted on the cane after he stitched her leg the second time, and both Vaughn and her father watched her carefully to make sure she was using it. She wasn't sure she liked being babied by her father, but she didn't fight it. Jack would never talk about his emotions, but his actions told her a great deal.

The rest of the team took their places at the table.

Nadia's usually erect posture was softened slightly. In the infirmary Sydney had seen the massive bruises across her midsection, souvenirs of her encounters with Lars and Hans. They were healing, but Sydney knew she was still in pain.

Vaughn sported a yellowing bruise on one temple, courtesy of George, who now resided in a maximum security federal penitentiary. His swift written promise of a guilty plea had earned him a solitary cell, where he felt safe from Soukis.

Sloane walked into the room, a self-satisfied smile on his face. His smug expression soured Sydney's outlook, but she remembered that she had promised herself she would try to control her attitude, if only for her sister's sake. She was learning how important family could be.

"Ladies and gentlemen," Sloane addressed the assembled team, "I have some good news. You all did exceedingly well on your recent mission. Our success helped avert a serious national crisis. And, as a by-product, provided Mr. Flinkman with a new device to study."

Marshall waved his hand at the mention of his name and smiled his thanks for the marvelous new toy.

"Mr. Carver is being transferred to his new home today, and Mr. Blake will be moving soon also. Though I don't imagine"—Sloane paused, smiling slightly—"they will be allowed visiting privileges."

Sloane dropped his jovial tone. "But enough of that," he said briskly. "I have another piece of news that I think will interest all of you."

Sydney and Nadia glanced at each other. Sloane continued.

"It seems that the cartel Mr. Soukis was involved with was not pleased with his failure. In fact, they had several billion reasons to be displeased. They were so unhappy that they removed him from his position as head of the cartel. Of course, the remaining members are now busy fighting over what's left—which should keep them busy for a long while."

He held up his hand to forestall any comment. "But that isn't the best news. It seems that somehow—we don't know how, but we have our suspicions—a couple of Russian officers found out about Soukis. They were guarding Blake, so the presumption is they got the information from him. While they lost their prisoner, the Russians were delighted to have evidence of Mr. Soukis's involvement."

Sloane glanced at his watch. "Even as we speak, the Russian authorities are taking Mr. Soukis into custody, at his dacha on the Black Sea."

Sydney glanced over at Dixon, who looked back impassively. She remembered their encounter with the Russian authorities, and with the two guards whom they had left on the banks of the Don, in their underwear.

Sydney winked at Dixon. Dixon gave a look of feigned innocence, which told her that he knew what she was thinking, though he would never admit it.

The meeting dissolved amid congratulations among the members of the team. They had done a good job, an important job, and done it well. As they made their way from the conference room back to their desks, Sydney hung back. She placed a hand on Dixon's arm, and he stopped, waiting beside her while the others moved out of the room.

When they were alone, Sydney looked her partner in the eye.

"Dixon, how are you doing? Is Steven okay?"

"Steven is a scared little boy, Sydney. I didn't realize how bad it was for him, but now I do. We're getting some help for him, and Robin and I are going to family counseling with him," Dixon said. He shook his head. "I should have done this a long time ago."

Sydney laid her hand over his. "But you are doing it now. You're making the effort. I believe it will all turn out right for the kids, and for you."

"It will." There was no hesitation, no question in Dixon's voice. He held his head high, and Sydney could see the confidence he had in himself, and his family.

"There are a lot of things I do for my family, Sydney. And this job is one of them. I go out there every day"—he nodded toward the city above them—"and I try to make it a better place for them. It's what we all do: you and Vaughn and Nadia; Marshall and Weiss and your father. Even Sloane, if you believe what he says. We make the world a better place for our children to live in. I just need to learn how to balance raising my kids and doing this job. It's no good to save hundreds—thousands—of lives if I don't save my kids, too."

Dixon stopped. He looked vaguely embarrassed that he had exposed so much of himself to Sydney.

Sydney looked even deeper into his dark eyes.

"You're doing the right thing, Dixon. You really are. Believe me, I know what a screwed-up childhood is like. And that's not what you're giving your kids. If the mistakes my dad made raising me, his failures and my problems, can help you avoid the same mistakes, then maybe they're worth something after all."

Before she could say anything more, Vaughn appeared at the door to the conference room. "Some of us are going to grab a bite," he said. "You guys want to come along?"

Dixon chuckled. "Not me. I got a couple of short people waiting at home who made me promise to bring home pizza and a movie." He patted Sydney's shoulder. "Good job, partner. Get some rest, okay? Glad to have you home." Then he left.

Vaughn cocked an eyebrow at Sydney. "You coming?"

Sydney started to say yes, but she hesitated. There was something she had to do first.

"I'll catch up," she said.

Vaughn didn't move. "You sure you don't want me to wait for you?"

"No, I'll be fine. I just have a couple of things to clear off my desk before I go," Sydney said.

"Well," Vaughn's voice still held a question, but he knew she wouldn't offer any more explanation. "If you say so," he said, and shrugged.

Sydney limped to her desk. Around her, members of the team were putting away files, locking desks, and shutting down computers. The mission was over.

Minutes later, alone in the silent office, Sydney cleared away the last of her files. She savored the rare moment of peace. As she put the last file in her desk drawer, a picture caught her attention. She pulled it out and looked at it.

It was a snapshot of her mother. A young and beautiful Irina smiled out at her, an infant cradled in her arms. Irina had told her the baby was her niece, but Irina had told her many things, and many of them were lies.

Sydney wondered who the baby was. She probably would never know. Irina had lived a life like Sydney's, had held a job like Sydney's, and had left behind two daughters. Two babies who had depended on her for everything. It may have been the bravest thing she had ever done. It also may have been the thing she regretted most.

Sydney didn't know if she would ever be able to

match her mother's courage—if she would ever be brave enough to have a child of her own. She didn't bother trying to come up with an answer. For now, just knowing the question was enough.